The Chronicles of Thomas Frith, O.P.

S.M.C.

2017
DNS Publication

The Chronicles of Thomas Frith, O.P. by S.M.C. was originally published in London in 1957 by Blackfriars Publications. This 2012 edition by DNS Publications contains the original text with the addition of translations of some of the Latin passages.

Printed in the United States of America

Nihil obstat: Daniel Duivesteijn, S.T.D.
Imprimatur: E. Morrogh Bernard
Vic. Gen.
Westmonasterii, die 24a Aprilis, 1957

DNS PUBLICATIONS
Dominican Nuns of Summit
543 Springfield Avenue
Summit, New Jersey 07901
www.nunsopsummit.org

ISBN: 0999243233
ISBN-13: 978-0999243237

FOREWORD

In dealing with historical persons I have done my best to keep to fact. These facts I have taken from Ferario's *De Rebus Hungariis* and Malvenda's *Amales*. Wherever there is a supposed copy from another manuscript, this is a translation from one of these two authors. I am also much indebted to Father Bede Jarrett's *English Dominicans*. The faults are all my own.

S.M.C.

Books by the Same Author

A Treasure of Joy and Gladness

And No Birds Sing

Angel of the Judgment

As the Clock Struck Twenty

Brother Petroc's Return

Children Under Fire

The Chronicles of Thomas Frith, O.P.

The Dark Wheel

The Flight and the Song

Henry Suso: A Saint and Poet

Jacek of Poland

Margaret, Princess of Hungary

Once in Cornwall

The Spark in the Reeds

Steward of Souls

Storm out of Cornwall

CONTENTS

CHAPTER I

Why I Wrote These Chronicles

My injured leg had been paining me all night. I was told that the wound from the fall had set up an ulcer which would not heal. I was tired but I could not rest so, after I had taken as much as I could of the bread and ale the infirmarian brought me, I dragged myself across the room to a patch of sunlight by the window and settled myself there, crouched in the warmth like a sick old dog. Those were the moments when I always found it difficult to keep the eye of my mind fixed outward.

I had been gritting my teeth because of the pain in my leg and saying my beads as well as I could for about an hour, when the infirmary door opened and the prior came in. Our prior is a big man with a big bass voice. He looked at me questioningly.

'How are you, Thomas?' was all he said, a very ordinary greeting, but the tone of his voice and the cheerful way he spoke brought something brisk and living into the room. One could not be sorry for oneself when the prior was within earshot. I blinked up at him from my patch of sunlight.

'I might be better and I might be worse, Father,' I said. 'The pain in my leg is—not pleasant.' That was all I meant to say, but somehow the rest followed; my real trouble, I mean, which was not my injured leg. 'The pain would be nothing if only I were able to work. For the last three months I have crawled from my bed to the window seat and from the window seat to my bed. I have rested as I was told to do, but I don't seem to be getting any better. I'm an old man I know, but not so old as to be past work. I've given the leg its chance, and now I'm in two minds whether to ask you to let me bandage it tight and take to the roads again. I'd rather die that way.'

The prior said nothing for a minute or two, but stood looking down at the sunshine on the floor and humming below his breath, like a great bumble bee.

'Didn't you travel east about thirty years ago, Thomas?' he asked presently.

I did not answer at once. I could not; for, at his words, the warmth of those three wonderful years so flooded my mind that I could only sit silent and bask in their memory, just as my old body was basking in the spring sunshine.

'Yes,' I said at last. 'I was in Poland in the summer of '57, in Prague for the following winter, in Hungary from the summer of '58 to that of '59, in Sandomierz during the winter of '59, then at Kracow in '60 until I came home in the summer.'

'I've been looking in the library and I can find no record of that journey of yours, though you were assigned here to Holborn on your return.'

I stared at the prior. What had he in his mind? Of course there was no written record, for as soon as I came back I was set to preaching all up and down East Anglia. There had been no time to talk about my journey, much less write about it. Besides after what I had seen of a Preacher's life abroad, I was interested in work, not in making records of what I had seen.

'And now, since you are tied by the leg and I am in no mind to allow you to bandage it and start tramping again, how would it be to use your hands for a change and write an account of those three years in the east? No'—as I was about to protest—'I know you have never written anything and it is late in life to begin now. But I am not asking for a history or treatise. Just jot down the memories of an old man as they come to you. Write it, not for the public, but for yourself and myself only. I'll tell the infirmarian to arrange some sort of a table and a rest for your feet. God be with you!'

He turned on his heel and walked out of the room, leaving me alight with interest and a certain fear. Our prior was like that.

The sun was higher now, shining through the budding green of the tree just outside the window; making quivering patterns like water on the wall. It was just so that the water had danced and quivered on that day when I stood looking out over Thames, and the tall seaman came up and stood beside me saying: 'Sir Friar, I once saw one of your sort, standing just like you are standing now; but *he* stood at the edge of a frozen sea, far away in the white north; a land where mid-summer is almost one long day and midwinter almost perpetual night.'

His ship was moored to the quay not far from where I was standing and he took me aboard, and I asked the Master to come back with me to Blackfriars, and he told us...

The door opened and the infirmarian came in with a big armchair. As he moved about the room settling the furniture, he was telling me something about a new law expelling the Jews from England; and of the death of Margaret of Norway, heiress to the Scottish throne. But, though I answered yes and no, more or less at random, my mind had really gone back thirty years. I had landed in London after the voyage from Danzig not long after our late king Henry had returned from signing the Peace of Paris; and now his son had been eighteen years on the throne and, if rumors were true, we were not far from war with France again.

The infirmarian went as far as the open door to fetch a small table-board and trestles, a rest for my leg, parchment, inkhorn, pens, and a writing board. He made me comfortable and I sat fingering the pens and thinking.

Details of those three years in the east began to come back to me, first one thing, then another in a series of pictures; one fading out and another taking its place, without much conscious volition on my part. Presently I made the effort to regain mastery of my thoughts and began to examine these memories. It seemed as though I might do something with them. I know I am not a writer, I told myself, but, since the prior wishes it, I can at least make some attempt to set down the pictures that I see in my mind, and the things that people said just as I can recall them. Of course what I write will probably differ in

4

some small details from what actually happened; things are very seldom comprehended completely objectively, everything is bound to be colored in some degree by the personality behind the mind which grasps them. But, if I am faithful to what I remember, the written word should closely approximate the truth.

However, though I had the materials, I did not begin to use them either that day or the next. I just sat with the parchment before me and allowed my mind pictures to grow clear. There were the places I had visited: the endless stretches of the Polish and Hungarian plains, the mountains of the Sudetan Alps, the long, broad stretches of river.

There were the people I had met: Jasek, whom they call Hyacinth over here; the giant Sadoc coming into the priory at Kracow, all windblown from the great plains; and little Margaret in her island home. There was the pupil of Master Albert and our journey to Prague; and Kazemierz, whom I only met once alive, but who played such a part in my thoughts and ideas. There was Bartholomew's tale of Kiev and of what the Tartars had left of its three hundred churches.

On the third day I began to write just as the prior had told me, a simple chronicle, not for the public, but for himself and myself alone. My writing resolved itself into word pictures, followed by blank spaces where my memory failed me; and sometimes I added my thoughts on the things which I had seen and heard, mostly puzzles. Some of these I solved and some will only be solved on the other side of death.

The language was at first a difficulty. I began to write in my native tongue, but I found this very hard, so I changed to Latin; for this was what we spoke together in the priories, and I find it easier to translate Polish and Hungarian into Latin than into English.

I have not gone back on what I have written for fear I should be tempted to tear it up. After all what is this chronicle but a series of jottings, random jottings.

Chapter II

About the Priory of St Thomas in the Far North

My real life began, though it was a long time before I
realized it, the evening that I met the sailor on the
Thames bank.

It was in the year 1257, the year after Richard of
Cornwall, our King Henry's brother, was elected
Emperor. I had just left Oxford where I had done well.
Looking back I can see what a self-satisfied young
jackanapes I was. My world was the Schools, and Oxford
the School of schools, and I could see nothing beyond.
Of course I had no idea how pleased I was with myself,
how intolerant of those whose ambitions turned
elsewhere. A chance meeting with a sailor led to the
change of all my values.

As I said before, he took me aboard his ship which
was unlading at the quay. The crew were in general tall
and blond, obviously Scandinavians, but the Master was
a small, sharp-faced Englishman; from Newcastle so the
sailor told me. He greeted me politely enough, but as if
his mind was elsewhere. I suppose it was, for the deck

was in confusion; bales of all kinds piled here and there, and men running everywhere, pulling and lifting and carrying things over the gangway to the wharf.

'Your man tells me that you have found a priory of Friars Preachers somewhere in the far north?' I said, wasting no words, for I saw that I should get nothing from him unless I told him at once what my errand was.

'That's true enough. We were blown out of our course and wintered there,' he answered. 'But if your Reverence will excuse me, I can't spare time to talk now, we are busy unloading the ship. We have to clear this cargo and take on a fresh one, tomorrow, ready to sail for Danzig early next week when wind and tide will serve.'

'Can't you find time to come up to Blackfriars Priory over there, on the north side of the river? Our prior is keen on hearing of new things, especially if they concern our own Order. Come to supper and spend the night there if you care to.'

'If things go well, I'll come up on Sunday evening,' he answered, and hurried off, leaving me to find my own way ashore. I went straight back and told the prior of what I had heard and of how I had invited the Ship Master to the Priory.

He came on Sunday afternoon as he had promised and, after he had had supper in the refectory, sitting next the prior, all the Brethren except those who had pressing duties elsewhere went to the guest hall. The Ship Master sat with the senior Fathers, upright and a little forward, with his hands palm to palm between his knees, very neat, like one accustomed to living in confined spaced. Later I saw many sailors sitting in the same fashion, but at the time it interested me much, for I had been bred inland and knew nothing about the sea or seafarers.

After he and the seniors had talked together quietly for a little while, the prior asked him to tell us all about our priory in the far north. The dusk was gathering as he began his story, sitting very still, his hands hanging limp between his knees and his elbows resting on them. As I was one of the youngest there I was sitting on the far side of the room just opposite him and, being fascinated, I noticed his stillness and the lack of any gesture, as he spoke slowly with little pauses and silences. This is what he told us:

'Late last autumn I was bound for Trondheim with a cargo from Newcastle. We ran into a strong gale and were blown off our course. I lost my bearings because the rain clouds by day and night covered the sun and the stars, so there was nothing for it but to run before the gale and hope for the best.

'When at last the gale had blown herself out, we found that we were not far from land; a rocky, indented shore, much like Norway. We made land at the mouth of one of the fjords where there was a little township. The people were kindly folk and many of them spoke Norse. They helped us to beach the ship in a sheltered inlet and promised that they would give us a hand with repairing her. Those we met were Christians and they told us that they have one bishop, and that the whole island is his diocese. They have no king, but rule themselves by means of a kind of Parliament they call the Allthing. The Parliament meets in the summer and as we were there through the winter only, I know no more about it; though

I have heard that they have so many disputes that little work is done in it.

'They told us that King Haco the Old of Norway has made several expeditions to the land, which they call Iceland in their own language, a very proper name. King Haco claims Iceland as part of the Kingdom of Norway. There are a few Norwegian settlers, otherwise the islanders are left to manage their own affairs, so they pay little heed to the king and his claims since these do not interfere with them.

'Our ship was so badly damaged and needed so much overhauling, that winter was on us in full force before we were ready to start. So we wintered there and set out again for Trondheim in the late spring. It is a wonderful island. There are mountains all on fire at their summits and springs of boiling water; some of these shoot up fountains of steam and boiling water into the air every fifteen minutes or so. In the winter the days grow shorter and shorter until the sun only shows low on the horizon for a short time at midday; in the height of summer the sun does not set for more than an hour or so. During the winter nights there is a wonderful blaze to the north, sometimes like a curtain of fire, sometimes like masses of streamers and shooting bands of light.

'When the work on the ship was well under way, we used to go ashore fairly often in twos and threes, to see the land around. One day Peter, my first mate, and I went farther than usual, and there on a headland, black against the white, stood a man looking out over the sea.

'The people were all so friendly that we made no difficulty about going up to him and, when we got near, we found that he was a Friar Preacher, just like one of yourselves. He spoke to us in Norse and, being a Newcastle man and travelling so often to Scandinavia, I do not find much difficulty in understanding a serviceable amount of the language.

'The friar told us that they had a house on the shores of the next bay some ten miles off, and invited us to come and see it. But I did not like two officers to be away from the ship so long without notice, so I asked him to excuse us for the moment, but that we would like to come later. He told me that any or all of us would be welcome. He said that the friars had come over from Norway, with the king on his visits, two or three at a time; that although the people were Christians and had a bishop of their own, they found there was work for them to do in Iceland and so they stayed on.

'A week or so later I went to visit the friar in his priory and saw some of the most wonderful things I have ever seen in all my roving life. The place was one story high, a proper monastery with cloisters and the like. It was built close to the shore, and there was a sizeable township grown up around it. Not far off there was a great snow-covered mountain, blazing away merrily at the top. Black pitch, or some such substance, pours down its sides and this hardens into rock. The friars had built their house of great slabs of this, mortared with pitch from a lake of the same stuff a short distance away. As the volcanic stone is porous, they had covered the walls and roof with a coating of the same, so that no damp could seep through.

'Quite close to the house were springs of hot water; one boiling, some hot and some fairly cool. They had dug channels from the boiling spring to their house and these channels run through it under the floor and keep it warm. They do all their cooking in the hot springs, even making bread there, for they have no other means of heating. The food is good. Some of the cooler streams are directed to the sea through the gardens, so that, summer and winter alike, you can always find fresh fruit and vegetables.

'We had our dinner in the refectory; bread—their bread is very good although it is cooked in such an outlandish fashion—and fresh fish of different kinds. The prior told me that the hot streams running into the bay prevent the sea freezing there and, as in consequence fish are plentiful in the bay, they can get as much as they need all the year round.

'After dinner we went into the garden, and it was wonderful to see how green it was; and little flowers too, small and shy-looking, but flowers all the same. After that, as long as we were in harbor, we saw quite a lot of the friars; our men went to the priory and the friars came to the ship.'

He stopped and looked round at us with those far-seeing eyes of his, crinkled at the corners. We stared back at him for a minute or two, digesting what he had told us, and then we began to ask him questions.

In answer he told us that the priory was dedicated to St Thomas and that, whenever weather served, the friars travelled over the island preaching. They had preached quite a number of times on board his ship, for most of the crew were Norwegians, and—the captain smiled a little wryly—they had not minced matters and, in the end, the whole ship's company had been to Confession. After all, he asked us, what can you expect when men are cast ashore on a strange land for months at a time? The women were not much to look at but...For my part, knowing how matters often stood even in England, I was not surprised.

There were lamps filled with whale and seal oil in the church, refectory and cloisters, he told us, nasty smelly things, but better than nothing. Yes, there were a few novices, Icelanders, and one of the friars was a Master in Theology and one or two more Lectors, so they had set up a small house of studies.

He stood up after this and said that he must be going back to his ship, for there was still a lot to be done. Then, looking straight at the prior, he made this offer:

'We go to Danzig next week and from there the Vistula carries boats right through to Poland. Your Order is doing a great work in that part of the world and if one of your men has a taste for travel, I can make room for him on board.'

'Thank you,' said the prior, 'that offer is too good to be missed.' And he looked round, his eye resting on one after the other of the community. At last it reached me and, with a sinking heart, I saw it light up.

'Thomas,' said the prior, 'have you ever been out of England?'

'No,' said I, 'but...' In a flash it all came back to me, how well I had done at Oxford, and how I had been told that I ought to be sent on to Paris and Bologna perhaps, afterwards. And now, there was the prior looking at me with a most unpleasant twinkle. No wonder I said 'but.' But he either did not, or would not hear it, for he went straight on: 'It is time, Thomas, that you learnt to be a little less insular. You will sail with the ship on—?' He looked towards the Master who promptly replied 'Tuesday.' 'From Danzig you will go down the river to Kracow. There you will put yourself under the obedience of the Polish Provincial. I will give you a letter telling him I have sent you to study—um—humanity, yes, humanity.' The twinkle in his eyes deepened. 'When he thinks you are ready, he can send you back and we will make a preacher of you.'

I made the *Venia* of course, there was nothing else for me to do. Then we left the guest hall.

I was feeling bitter. My studies finished. No Professor's chair for me. Ever. Just to preach up and down the country to ignorant peasants. Me! My hardly won knowledge wasted on.... It did not bear thinking about. I had to do as I was told. I began to gather my things together.

I was very young in those days.

CHAPTER III

I Go to Poland

We set sail on Tuesday. Our cargo consisted of fleece for Danzig. Now, although my father was a master weaver and I had been brought up, so to speak, in the midst of wool, I have always hated the smell of it; so, between the close cramped quarters aboard and the oily smell of the bales of fleece, I began to be very sea-sick before we were even clear of Thames. No one bothered much about me, they were all too busy, so, after one glance into the hold, packed and reeking, I found a corner between two bales of linen stuff on deck, and lay there, trying to forgive the prior and waiting for death.

We rolled and pitched over the North Sea, round Denmark and across the south Baltic; and all I remember is a seemingly endless time of misery, punctuated by short periods of comparative peace, when we called at some port and I was able to sit up on deck and eat and drink something.

The first clear picture in my mind is of our reaching smooth water at last and of my standing, weak and dizzy, leaning against the port rail and staring at a huddle of houses; warehouses, dwelling houses and wharfs, sliding down, as it seemed, right on to the sandy reaches of mud flats, not altogether unlike our Essex marshes.

There was a clean purged look about everything, for the air was clear and the sky blue and cloudless. One of the crew brought me something to eat and drink, and afterwards the captain came to tell me that I must leave the ship, and that he would send someone to take me to our priory in the town. There they would arrange for me to go down the Vistula to Kracow by boat. He had to unlade, take on a fresh cargo and be ready to sail for England as soon as possible.

In one respect alone Danzig is specially memorable to me, for it was at Danzig that I first heard of Jasek.

I thanked the Master and followed my guide through the town. I do not think that I really remember much about Danzig. After living three years in eastern Europe it would be easy to imagine what I saw, but I seem to remember nothing much except watching my step and trying to get used to walking on firm ground again. Besides my stay in the city was so short that the handsome austere pile of the priory is the only clear thing in my mind.

I had to wait a couple of days for a boat to take me on and the community was very kind to me. The language was no great difficulty, for we all spoke Latin. During the time I was there I learnt a little about the place.

Jasek, it appears, had first brought the friars to Danzig and had told the few travel-worn men that before

long they would have an important priory there. Of its
importance there could be no doubt. Jasek had been back
to see them twice or three times since. That was all which
could be expected from a man who had travelled as far
as the Great Wall of China, and had built a large priory
in the now ruined city of Kiev. Why ruined? Did I not
know about the Tartar invasion? They were much
surprised at my ignorance. Perhaps I had not heard of
Jasek either? That was also strange. He was one of the
greatest men of the Order and his journeying over
eastern Europe and Asia were mapped out by the priories
he had built. The Great Wall of China meant nothing to
me, so I did not question the possibility of Jasek reaching
it among so many other places.

Danzig was not an easy place to live in, so they said.
The Teutonic Knights were aggressive and overbearing,
thought the world had been made for them. But one
must not complain, for they did not interfere seriously
with the friars. Things would be very different, of course,
if the Preachers had not been directly under the
jurisdiction of the Pope and exempt from the authority
of the bishops. For instance, Jasek's uncle, Bishop Ivo,
had been sent into exile some seven or eight years after
they had gone with him to Kracow. But it had made no
difference to the position of the friars, nor to the esteem
in which they were held.

The Teutonic Knights? Did I know nothing about
those? In the first place they had been a crusading Order
like the Templars. When they found that there was no
longer work for them to do in the south, they had turned
their thoughts to the conquest and conversion of the
heathen Prussians; rather more conquest than

17

conversion. Still they had done a big work in subduing a ferocious people, and the Poles found them useful neighbors on their northern boundaries.

I reached Danzig on a Wednesday and set off again early on the following Friday. The prior and another came down to the river wharf, to see me on board and wish me God-speed. If you stop at Sandomierz, they told me, be sure to visit our house there. You will like Sadoc the prior. They spoke to the ship master about it and he promised that I should land at Sandomierz.

The boat was broad and flat with several pairs of oars. The water was smooth and I almost enjoyed the journey. As they rowed, the men sang; a doleful ditty on four or five notes, very monotonous and seemingly endless. Poland is a great plain. I used to think East Anglia flat after the Peak country where I was bred, but it is nothing to this. The only break in its expanse is made by huge forests; sometimes black on the horizon, sometimes stretching great arms down to the water's edge. We stopped at various small towns and villages on the way and I used to get out to stretch my legs and look at the wooden houses and listen to the creak-creak of the wooden wheel which pumps water from the village well. One heard it in every village and it was as unending as the boatman's song. The river went on and on, and the song went on and on, and, on every side, the plain stretched on.

I found the Polish language very strange. German is guttural, French is crisp and crackling, but Polish sounds so like ours that it comes as a surprise when one finds one cannot understand a word. One feels somehow as though one ought to understand. We were on the river five days and during the whole time I was unable to speak a word to anyone.

On the fifth day we came to the huddled wooden mass of Sandomierz and the boat-master came to me and made signs that I was to follow him.

Though in England our smaller dwelling houses are often built of wood, our churches and monasteries are of stone. Here churches and monasteries are generally made of wood. Our priory was dedicated to St Mary Magdalen, there was another dedicated to St James. We had two in the one town. The porter took me to the prior, Father Sadoc, a large grizzled old man not unlike a lion, but with a massive head and a benevolent face. He greeted me kindly, blessed me and told the porter to find someone to show me round. He was sorry he could not take me himself, but he was off on business that afternoon. The porter was old and garrulous and as soon as we were outside the door he stopped to tell me about the prior.

'He is a very great man,' he said. 'He was sent to Hungary with the Blessed Father Paul by our Father Dominic himself. After some time he was sent to Poland, where he built this great house. Counting the novices, we are forty-nine in community. Father Paul was killed by the Tartars in the great invasion.'

'Father Sadoc is a great preacher?' I asked.

'Indeed he is,' answered the porter. 'Here, there and everywhere. Now I'll tell you what happened when he was a young man on his way east from Bologna. He, Paul and a third, Beranger, stopped to preach at the Benedictine School of Studies at Lorch in Austria. As a result, three students offered themselves as novices. That night, the devil appeared to our prior. "Woe to you," he said. "You have come to drive us from our possessions. And it is these children who will drive us out.'"

This was my first experience of something which used often to exasperate me. Poland was full of missionaries, great men of ours who had travelled hundreds of miles and converted thousands, and when one asked about them, their work was dismissed in a sentence as a mere matter of routine, and one was fobbed off with some tale of a miracle or devil.

The porter handed me over to a young friar newly ordained and he took me round the priory and I spoke to a number of men. When these heard that I was a stranger, an Englishman, on my way to Kracow, they spoke at once of Jasek and his elder cousin, Ceslas, dead about fourteen years. But I only heard fragments as everyone seemed to take it for granted that I knew all about them; fragments and miracles. One story stuck in my memory.

Jasek had been preaching in the country west of Kiev when he decided to go on pilgrimage to Kracow, as it was the feast of the Translation of St Stanislaw and the martyr had been buried at Kracow. This meant Jasek crossing the Vistula, and when he reached the river bank he found a large group of people collected around the body of a young nobleman, named Peter de Proschovo, who had fallen from his horse into the river and been drowned.

The dead man's mother, the Lady Falislava, was there, and as soon as she saw Jasek she ran to him and, falling at his feet, cried out:

'Father Jasek, man of God, I know that you are a devoted servant of God, full of kindness and mercy. I am a widow and this is my only son. What can I do?'

Jasek told her to wait a little and then he went a short distance off and knelt down and prayed. When he came back, he asked the lady: 'Daughter Falislava, when was your son drowned?'

The mother said: 'He was drowned last evening, but we did not find the body until this morning.'

Then Jasek knelt beside the body and took the dead hand in his. 'Peter,' he said, 'in the name of Our Lord Jesus Christ, in whose name I preach, through the intercession of the Blessed Virgin Mary may you receive life.' The young man sat up at once alive and well.

The man who told me reeled off the names of a number of people who had seen the miracle. But when I asked where Jasek had been preaching, whom he had been preaching to and how many conversions he had made, he just shrugged his shoulders. Preaching and conversions were routine work, just a man's job; nothing specially exciting.

We ended our tour by going round the church and up the tower, where we sat in one of the window slits and talked. Although he was called Kazemierz, my friend was not Polish. He was a young Gascon, the page of some nobleman who had joined King Louis of France in Palestine. When the King returned to France in '54, Kazemierz travelled north, visited Constantinople and, joining a party of merchants, finally found himself in Sandomierz.

As we sat, looking down on the city and the great stretch of country beyond, the broad river and the blue sky, drinking in the keen fresh air, we talked of this and that. Kazemierz, the knight's son, said that he found in the friar's life his ideal of chivalry.

'Francis of Assisi vowed himself to the Lady poverty,' he said. 'And we have vowed ourselves to the Lady Truth. It is a great thought. For Truth means not only truth in word, but truth in ourselves; and so fidelity to her means also fidelity to God himself, the very Truth.'

This idea made no particular appeal to me, for being only the son of a Master Weaver, chivalry was not in my line. My ideal was good workmanship and a Master Craftsman to look up to and follow, so I told him that, for my part, I had always carried in my mind the old Saxon poem *The Dream of the Rood*, and of how God, our Savior, was the young Hero who mounted the Tree of the Cross as his royal throne. There he was, high as heaven above us; raised not only by the greatness of his Divinity, but also by his unparalleled suffering, so that I can only look up from my littleness and worship. God the Son was my Master Craftsman, and I was only his least apprentice.

Kazemierz stared at me, but made no comment. 'I am looking for a Lady,' he said quietly, 'and Truth is she. As her knight, I serve her, but she is so high above me that I can only offer my humble service at a distance.'

I smiled. 'Our object is the same: humble worship. But we have different approaches.'

Presently we found ourselves discussing miracles. My companion said that the whole thing had always been something of a puzzle to him; not the miracle in itself, but the working of them, which seemed to him to imply a species of intimacy with God that he could not understand.

'God is the Creator of the world,' said Kazemierz, 'and God the Son has redeemed us. By the very facts of creation and redemption, they are raised so infinitely above us, the created and redeemed, that I can only hide my face and adore in humility. And yet, you should hear some of ours! If they don't get what they ask for they positively scold God Almighty. And the strangest part of all is that he actually seems to approve of it and gives them what they are bullying him for.'

I said that, as far as I was concerned, I found some of these miracles almost impossible of belief. But, given the reality of the miracle, then people like the Poles, passionate and in some ways almost childish, were the people to work them.

Then we both laughed saying that we were rationalists and skeptics, and that it was as well that none of the seniors had heard us or we should have been excommunicated on the spot.

It was time to get back to the boat and we came down the tower steps. At their foot, just as one turned into the church, hung a large crucifix. It was set so low that I stood almost on a level with the arms; and the hanging Figure was torn and bloodstained to a dreadful degree. I stopped in front of it.

'There,' I said pointing to it, 'is the difference between these eastern people and us westerners. Think of our Crucifixes, high above us and idealized and then look at that. That is how they work their miracles; and that way is neither for you nor for me.'

We did not say much more as we walked back to the boat and Kazemierz saw me aboard. We promised to pray for each other.

That was the first and last time that we met alive. But the man remained to me a vivid memory; partly, I am afraid, because I felt hot and ashamed to think of what I had said to him: things that I had never said before even to myself.

CHAPTER IV

Kracow and Jasek

I reached my journey's end at last and one afternoon, a day or so later, we moored 'longside a jetty, and the skipper took me to the priory which was almost on the river edge. When one first catches sight of them, the Church and Priory of the Holy Trinity take one's breath away; for in this land of wooden buildings, both are of stone, so that the effect of this great stone pile in the midst of wooden houses is quite overwhelming. I learnt later that the church was given and the priory built for the friars in '22 by the bishop, his Chapter and the chief men of Kracow.

The provincial was at home and I gave him my prior's letters. He read them, glanced at me with a queer, one-sided little smile, and said: 'So you are to study Humanity, not Divinity. We will do the best we can for you.' Then turning to the porter who was standing at the door, he went on: 'Find Father Thomas a student's room and tell one of the younger men to look after him.'

25

I stammered my thanks and followed the porter out. It was exceedingly kind of the provincial to give me a room to myself, instead of a cell in the common dormitory, shut off from one's next-door neighbors, but open to the corridor. I had not expected this.

A pleasant young brother took me down to supper which followed almost immediately. I drank my wine and ate bread and a queer tasting cheese, listening to the reader, and glancing round from time to time at the smooth round heads and rather impassive faces of the community: all strangers, all men of an alien race. I felt like a lone starling in a parliament of rooks; only the starling would have had more self-possession.

We had just finished None next day and were coming through the cloister, when there was a stir among those in front of me and I heard someone say: 'Jasek has come home again.'

The seniors pressed forward, and as we happened to be opposite a doorway, those around me turned and went out on to a kind of portico with wooden seats. One of them took me by the arm and drew me out with them. They seemed both pleased and amused.

'Did you hear that Jasek is at home again?' said one.

'Where has he come from?' asked another.

'Halicz. The Duke sent for him, and as our priory there is under the patronage of the Duke we must be friendly. But dining with the great is not a business which would appeal to our Jasek.'

'I suppose that he stayed at the priory. It must be about nineteen years old. I know he has urgent business here and would hurry back, but all the same he has returned extraordinarily soon. I wonder how he managed it?'

'Do you mean to say that you've lived here five years off and on and you ask such a question? River walking, my dear man. Where are your wits?'

This was too much for me. I pulled the sleeve of the man next me. 'River walking?' I asked. 'What on earth is that?'

There was a chorus of laughter.

'Of course,' said my neighbor. 'Thomas does not know our Jasek. When you have been here a little longer you will know that water is one of the many things that are no obstacle to him. When he comes to a river, he either spreads his cappa and sails over it, or makes the Sign of the Cross and walks over dry-shod.'

Said another: 'It's sober fact. Listen and I'll tell you something. He with some others were once due to preach in Plocenza, across the Vistula. When they got to the river, there was no boat in sight. This was serious because they were already on the late side and there was no time to wait for a boat. Jasek turned to the others and said: "Brothers, let us ask the Omnipotent God, who rules heaven and earth and sea, to allow us to cross this deep, rapid river." He knelt down for a minute and then made the Sign of the Cross over the water. "Follow me," he said to the others and started to walk over the river just as though it had been solid ground.

'But the others did not attempt to follow him; they told us afterwards that they simply dared not. So Jasek came back and spread his cappa on the water. "This," he said, "is the bridge of Jesus Christ. Step on it and do not be afraid." With Jasek standing over them they no more dared refuse to get on the cappa than they had dared cross the river alone after him. So they all stepped aboard. And they crossed the Vistula on that cappa as easily as if it had been a raft; and what is more, they were in time for their sermons in Plocenza.'

'What about that time they had to leave Kiev?' asked another. 'Jasek had built a large priory in Kiev and between '36 and '41, he made it his headquarters. Then came the great Tartar invasion under Ogdai and the community had to leave Kiev and come back to Kracow. Jasek was just finishing Mass when word was brought that the enemy were in the city. So he took the Blessed Sacrament and led the brethren out of the church. A man who was actually there told me this.

'There was a big statue of Our Lady at the bottom of the church, and, as Jasek passed, the statue said: "Jasek, my son, do not leave me." Jasek stopped, looked up at the statue and said something that my friend couldn't catch. Then the statue said again: "My Son will lighten the load." So Jasek took the great statue—you can see it in our church here, the one in the Lady Chapel to the right of the Sanctuary—and carried it in his left arm while he held the ciborium in his right hand. "In this way," said my friend, "he led us down to the Dnieper, told us to spread our cappas on the water and we sailed over dry-shod. Of course on the far side of the river we were in comparative safety."'

I made a movement, but before I could speak the friar, reading my thought, said: 'Why did we leave Kiev instead of remaining to take what was coming to us, as so many of our brethren in Hungary did? Well, most of the Christians in Kiev had been converted to the Greek Orthodox Church, and one never knew where their hatred for us Roman Catholics might lead them when they had the chance to injure us. And for Christians to kill Christians would have been a great scandal. By the way, Jasek left his footprint on the mud where they crossed the river and it can be seen to this day.'

Without giving me time to take breath, another broke in: 'What about the idol on the island, if Thomas has a taste for odd things?'

'Yes, that is a strange tale. We had it from some peasants who actually saw it happen. Jasek was preaching somewhere in the countryside not far from here, and he was doing little good; people came and listened to him, but he could make no headway with them. He began to search for the cause and soon found out that there was an island in the river where there was a grove with an idol. The people were worshipping there in secret and that was why Jasek was making no conversions. Naturally no boatman would take him out, so he walked to the island and destroyed the idol. On his way back the devil in the likeness of a man, came out of a thicket on the island and rushed across the water to him. "Miserable Jacako," shouted the devil. "What makes you drive me away from these places where I have ruled in peace?" Jasek made no answer, he just rushed at the devil brandishing his staff, and the fiend fled away at once.'

There was a pause. They looked at me and I looked at them. Were they in jest or earnest? Were they telling me facts, as they believed them, or plumbing my simplicity by a series of tall stories? Their faces told me nothing. In every way I was at a disadvantage.

Trying to look as impassive as my companions, I asked quietly: 'Except for these stories, is nothing known of Father Jasek's preaching and the conversions he has made? Is there no record of his journeys?' Without a pause one of them answered in a breath:

'We know that he has travelled through Pomerania and Prussia, Denmark, Sweden and Norway; afterwards he went south to Red and Black Russia; with Kiev as the novitiate, he founded a large Russian Province. After that he went north again to Prussia and east to Tartary. He went south to the Black Sea and from there east to the Indus and the Himalayas, to Tibet and as far as the Great Wall of China. Now he has just come back through Tartary, and on his way visited Russia for the third time.'

I said nothing. What could I say? I had asked for facts and I had been handed this. A man needed the forty league boots to carry out such a journey. I laughed. They looked at me coldly. Did they really believe this fairy tale? It was all beyond me and I had done the wrong thing to laugh. To my relief a brother came out and told one of the young men that the prior wanted him and, exclaiming at the lateness of the hour and wondering what the Master of Students would say about the time they had wasted, the whole group hurried indoors.

I followed them slowly, feeling puzzled and disgusted. Could it be that this Jasek, in spite of the reverence in which he was so obviously held, was no more than a trickster? And as for these young men, so smooth, so courteous, so well poised, so sure of themselves, what was going on in their sleek round heads?

On my way to the library, I happened to pass the subject of my cogitations; Jasek, a tall thin old man with a weather-beaten face. His habit was old and ragged, his shoes a ruin, but there was a brightness about him and a youthful gaiety which drew me to him in spite of myself and my prejudices. Assuredly, one could not dislike or despise Jasek.

He stopped and spoke, his face lit up with a smile.

'So you are Thomas, the young Englishman with your life before you, an exile in a foreign land and learning to preach. I am Jasek, the old Pole, who has finished his preaching, and has come home to die. May God bless you.' And he passed on.

In the course of a few days I made the acquaintance of a young German friar, a disciple of Master Albert of Cologne, himself another Albert. He had come to teach the elements of Philosophy and science to the students in the Kracow priory, who were to be sent later to study at the universities of Bologna and Paris, for there was no lack of brains among these young men. They were to have the chance which had been denied me, and I could not help envying them. How would they have taken it if, instead of their years of study in the university, they were to be shipped off to England to study Humanity instead of the Humanities?

A kind of friendship soon grew up between Albert and myself. We were both strangers and foreigners, and that made a link between us. We were both from the west and so we could understand one another. I found the Polish friars remained as great a mystery as ever; in some ways so smooth and polished and in others very youthful and passionate; quick to join in friendship, quick to take offense. They were fanatically independent. I once met a man carrying a heavy faggot of wood and suggested to him an easier way of managing the load. I learnt my lesson so well that I never made another suggestion. They could break their stubborn proud backs as far as I was concerned. They would get no more advice from me.

It was the same in politics and the larger issues. Though at the moment Kracow and Sandomierz were united in the Kingdom of Little Poland under the prince Boleslaw the Chaste and his Hungarian wife, Kinga, there was no guarantee of their remaining so, for the government and even the composition of the Provinces changed like the clouds on a windy day.

It seemed to me extraordinary that the Poles could stand religious obedience, for they were so touchy about their liberty. Yet the majority of them were certainly both good and obedient religious.

Chapter V

How Jasek Met Our Father Dominic

It happened one day that I was sent out with a friar who was to preach in the cathedral. He preached of course in the vernacular, and I sat on the steps of the pulpit and listened to his impassioned flow of words in a strange language. It was not by any manner of means the first time that I had been a preacher's companion, but in England I could follow what he was saying and take mental notes of the sermon. Here I could only watch the congregation and, to judge by their rapt faces, they were finding the matter absorbing. It was at times like this that the veil lifted a little and I had a glimpse of the man behind the Pole.

On coming back I glanced into the cloister garden and saw Jasek seated on a bench in the sunshine, with a group of young men on the ground at his feet. One of them caught sight of me and called me to join them. So I went out and sat among them on the grass. They talked of this and that for a few moments, and I watched the old man's face with its smile and the inward glow that lit it up.

Presently, one of the young men said: 'Father, tell Thomas the story of how you met our Father Dominic.'

'It is always good to talk of him,' he said and the glow on his face deepened giving it somehow a look of agelessness. It was as though Jasek were rejoicing in a foretaste of heaven. Then he began to speak, slowly and with pauses. Sometimes one of the men asked a question which he answered. And sometimes again he sat silent as though his mind had travelled right back to those days thirty-seven years before. I will give you his story consecutively because, unless you could see Jasek, you could not understand how pregnant these silences were.

'Ceslas and I were canons of our uncle Ivo's cathedral church. Ceslas, my cousin, had studied in Bologna. I had been to Prague and Bologna also. Ivo was obliged to go to Rome on business and he took us with him as well as two more of his men; Henry of Moravia and Herman the Teutonic. We had none of us, except Ceslas, been to Rome before, so we made the usual round; visited the churches and had an audience with the Pope.

'But these are things that everyone does who visits Rome, and at the moment there was other, more exciting, business on hand which was creating a stir in the city. There were several convents in the place and the nuns there were living an almost secular life. They often wore worldly clothes, paid and received visits, and would have been better outside a convent altogether.

'Our Father had just come to Rome after founding our nuns' priory in Prouille, and the Pope asked him to undertake the reform of those in Rome. As far as possible he was to gather the more fervent in one convent. So he went to the different convents in question and saw the nuns privately and together, and finally the most important of them, Santa Maria de Trastevere, agreed to accept enclosure and monastic observance.

'The first Wednesday in Lent, after the distribution of Ashes, was the day agreed on when a delegation of Cardinals with our Father were to meet the Abbess and the community in their Chapter House, the final details were to be agreed on and signed and the Abbess was to resign her office. Cardinal Orsini, a friend of my uncle's, was one of the delegates chosen and he invited my uncle with us four young men.

'We were most anxious to go. For one thing, our Father himself was a seven days' wonder in Rome, and for another thing, the excitement about the nuns ran high. Some were all for the reform, but many threatened to carry the nuns from their new monastery by force if our Father had his way.

'But, when we got there, something far more exciting drove the nuns and their affairs out of everyone's mind and the business of reorganization and enclosure was carried through without any difficulty. We went into the Chapter House where our Father and the nuns were already seated. I was in the background some distance off, of course, so I was able to study our Father without being seen. I have never seen anyone like him. He was a fair Spaniard; his hair was the color of ripe wheat—auburn, our Sister Cecilia used to call it—his complexion

35

almost that of a northerner; but under all glowed the rich, warm blood of the south. His expression was kindly and serene, with a glint of laughter somewhere at the back, and we men were drawn to him at once. He had a way with men.

'Business had hardly begun when a man came in posthaste and said something to Cardinal Orsini. The Cardinal seemed to ask a question or two, looking shocked and distressed. Then he turned to our Father and was beginning to say something, when quite suddenly he crumpled up on the floor. Our Father sprinkled him with holy water, helped him to his feet, and when he had recovered they all went on to the piazza outside. As we followed, the news was passed from one to the other: the Cardinal's nephew, Napoleon by name, had been thrown from his horse, dragged some distance on the ground, and killed.

'Our Father stood for a few minutes looking down at the poor fellow. The body was terribly mangled. Then several of the bystanders lifted the corpse and carried it into a room near the convent, and our Father spoke to one of his companions who hurried away. Word went round that he was going to say Mass in the nuns' church and we all followed him there.

'He vested and began, briskly but with great reverence; and when it came to the Consecration I saw him raised an arm's length above the ground. That is a fact and no imagination of mine, for we all saw it. Then he raised the Sacred Host in Elevation and sometimes even now at Mass I fancy I can still see it, held between those long tapering fingers. For our Father's hands were beautiful.

'When Mass was ended, our Father went back to the room where they had taken the body. It looked even more twisted lying on the bier. We all followed him; we could not help it, we had to see the end. Three times our Father knelt down and prayed and three times he stood up and bent over the body, straightening the limbs. After the third time, he made a large sign of the cross on the forehead and then raised his hands in prayer. Again we all saw him raised an arm's length above the ground. Suddenly he cried aloud: "Young man, Napoleon, in the name of our Lord Jesus Christ, I say to you arise!"

'Instantly the dead man sat up. It is a terrible thing to see someone raised from the dead. "Father, give me something to eat and drink," he said. Our Father helped him to his feet and he was completely whole and sound, without the slightest scar or blemish. "Come with me," said our Father, "and I will give you something to eat." The two went out together and Cardinal Orsini followed. We were left behind, stunned and bewildered.

'But in that hour, our Father had done more than raise the dead to life. At the moment when I saw him lifted up in ecstasy, he had drawn my soul to him and I knew that I must follow him to my life's end. There was to be no more studious dignity in a canon's stall for me; my life for the future must be one of preaching as his was. Ceslas said afterwards that he had felt just the same, and so did the other two. Our Father had a way of his own with men, even though Ceslas and I were no longer young.

'Next day Bishop Ivo went to St Sixtus to see him and took us with him. He had a request to make; he wanted a band of friars to go back to Poland with him. "I will see to it that they have a home and a church," said my uncle. But our Father shook his head, for he had only just sent away all that he could spare. Then his eye fell on the four of us. I made a move forward and then hung back; I was longing to offer myself, but felt it presumptuous to take the initiative before this servant of God. The others said afterwards that they had felt the same. We were on fire to offer ourselves, but were ashamed of our unworthiness. Our Father smiled a little as though he read our thoughts: "Give me these clerics of yours," he said in that resonant musical voice of his. "I will take them, train them and send them to you in Poland when I have made Friars Preachers of them." Assuredly our Father had a way with all men.

'For some months, then, we lived with our Father at St Sixtus and caught as best we could some sparks of his burning love for God and souls. We learnt from him to pray and to preach and then we left Rome.'

The old Friar sat silent for a moment or two and then rose and went slowly into the house. I watched him out of sight and then looked round at the others. They were all watching me.

'And ever since then,' I murmured half to myself, 'he has been teaching heathen and savages.'

'Not by any means. Jasek has had dealings with all the great folk in Poland, Austria, Prussia and around Kiev. He does his duty by them, but the poor, the ignorant and the heathen are the people that he loves most.'

'Who was he before he joined our Father?'

'He was one of the Odrowatz, as great a family as you may find in Poland. His father, Eustace, was famous as a soldier fighting against the Lithuanians and Prussians.'

'If his uncle the Bishop was also an Odrowatz that explains why they were both given canons' stalls.'

'Not at all, Bishop Ivo was no nepotist. Both Jasek and Ceslas were university men and had taken their Doctorate in both Theology and Canon Law.'

'What a waste it seems for two such brilliant and learned men to have frittered away their talents in missionary work among barbarians. Surely it would have been better for them to teach and train other, less gifted men, as missionaries.' I was voicing, in reality, a private complaint of my own.

'It is easy to see, Thomas, how young and inexperienced you are.' I jumped to hear a strange voice just behind me; the rather gruff tones of one of the Professors whom, so far, I had only seen from a distance.

'I know I am all that,' said I, 'but in what way have I just shown it?'

The newcomer gave a short laugh. 'Because you don't yet know that anyone with a certain amount of knowledge and a modicum of training can preach to scholars. If he chances to make a mistake he will not go far before someone points his error out to him. When it comes to teaching people who know nothing, then only the best is good enough. If the preacher should slip up, there is no one to put him right; and then one of two things is bound to happen. Either his catechumens remain in error, material heretics; or another missionary follows who preaches true doctrine; and the poor ignorant folk, their faith in their teacher shattered, do not know which to believe. I speak from experience, Thomas, to preach to ignorant people and barbarians is both humbling and frightening.'

He glanced round the group of us and then passed on. The young men looked at each other and at me.

'Phew!' said one.

'Who was that?' I asked in rather a small voice, for I was feeling considerably crushed. 'I have seen him about, but have not heard him speak.'

'That is a very important person. Although he generally talks as if he were in the Master's chair, there is always good sense at the back of what he says. He used to be one of Father Jasek's chief missionaries, and his frequent companion when he was younger; and what he does not know about missionary work is not worth knowing. He has the training of us. His chief business is to make us feel small. And he does this work most competently.'

CHAPTER VI

The Passing of Father Jasek

I can remember little more of importance happening until July drew to an end and, as August came in sweltering, with a dry hot wind blowing across the plains, it was not difficult to see that Father Jasek was failing rapidly. He was bent nearly double and began to walk with a stick; creeping from his cell to the church and back again. In fact, he seemed to spend the greater part of the day in the choir; his bent figure could be seen there at all hours, kneeling or standing before the altar. Daily his face grew more transparent and in some fashion ageless, his smile more radiant.

On August 4th as we sang his Office— I reckoned that it must be twenty-three years from the Canonization of our Father Dominic—something happened to Jasek as he was saying Mass. He was not ill, but he took nearly twice as long as he was accustomed. All was as usual until just after the Elevation, when he stopped and remained for quite quarter of an hour motionless with his arms extended. His head was thrown a little back and I can only describe his face as shining. I was kneeling not far behind and I thought, though I could not be perfectly sure, that I saw the ground under his feet.

Afterwards it was whispered around the community that Jasek had seen in a vision the Assumption of Our Lady. He had seen her crowned, surrounded by all the host of heaven; and afterwards, she had taken the crown from her head and shown it to him, saying: 'This crown is for you.' I know this for fact because it was Jasek himself who had told of the vision, when the prior asked him why he had been so long saying Mass; otherwise we should never have known, for the old missioner was not given to talking about himself.

Everybody, however, was talking about Jasek, for they all saw how frail he had grown; and the vision he had seen was, they thought, a warning that he was soon to die. The whole community had a singular affection for him and so they discussed his life and work and, in the fashion to which I was growing accustomed without liking it any better, it was of his miracles and not of his journeys and preaching that they spoke. For instance, one man told me:

'When I was assigned to Kiev, I think it was at the time when Jasek was there, just as we were going on a preaching mission, a lady—Clementia of Kosczjeliecz was her name and she was a great benefactor of the Order—asked him to come and spend the feast of St Margaret with her. She had been so good to us that Jasek did not like to refuse. The night before we started there was a terrific storm with such heavy hail that, next morning as we left the town and reached the countryside, we saw all the corn fields round us battered to the ground and the crops entirely ruined.

'I was not much looking forward to our visit under the circumstances, for Lady Clementia was a great landowner and she would be in terrible distress. I don't like crying women. Sure enough, before we reached the house, she came running out to meet us, crying as I had feared and wringing her hands. "Blessed Father Hyacinth," she cried out as soon as she had set eyes on us, "what wrong have I done? I asked you to visit me that you might give me spiritual comfort, and now, in great sorrow of mind and heart, I am coming out to you for material comfort. In an hour all the corn I have in my fields has been beaten down and destroyed. Please pray for me." Jasek tried to comfort her and by the time we had reached the house, a whole crowd of the neighboring farmers was waiting there for us.

'They ran up and surrounded the Father, calling out: "Jasek, holy Father Jakata, Father Jaczko, you are a man of faith, powerful in work. If you do not help us we shall die of hunger, for, as you see, the hail has destroyed all our crops. Pray for us, for we know that God hears all your prayers."

'They were all shouting at once, but that is more or less what I gathered from the babel. And Jasek was saying: "There, There!" in a comforting fashion and trying to soothe them. At last, when he could make himself heard, he said: "Dear sons, do not be disturbed, try to be resigned to this trial, for God, who forgives you all your sins, will comfort you. Do as I tell you. Go back to your homes and spend the night in prayer."

'Jasek never tells people to do things unless he does them himself, so he and I kept vigil too. I had the work of a life trying to keep awake for we had had a heavy day; but Jasek knelt upright the whole night through. And there was no question about his praying.

'From a window in the hall I saw the sun rise and then I heard a chorus of excited cries as a whole crowd of men threw open the door and came pouring in. Father Jasek scrambled rather stiffly to his feet as they pressed round him on all sides, seemingly half beside themselves with joy and excitement. I walked to the door and looked out, and I could hardly believe my eyes, for the whole countryside lay green and gold in the bright sunshine. Never in my life have I seen better crops. Jasek told them to thank God and then slipped away.'

Another told me: 'A cousin of mine, Felicia Gruszouska, had been married for twenty years and there had been no family. Her husband was furious because there was no heir, and he made my poor cousin suffer for her failure. She used to come to Jasek for help and advice. One day when life had been even more unbearable than usual and she had been publicly insulted by her husband, she came crying to the Father. She told me this herself; naturally it was not Jasek who broke confidence. She asked him what she could do. She said: "My husband and his friends make a laughing stock of me because I have no children. I know that God can do all things; that he has brought forth all things out of nothing, that he can make the barren fruitful. He is your Friend. Pray for me." She said that Hyacinth blessed her and told her to go home in faith and hope that she should have a son who would be the ancestor of bishops and noblemen. The son was born in due course and is now a fine young man; so my cousin is perfectly sure that the rest of the promise will be fulfilled.'

And so it went on. I heard stories without end, but when I asked for facts of his journeys and preaching, I got no more than a list of places and some statistics as to the number of conversions, if as much as that. It used to annoy me until I was almost angry with Father Jasek himself; and then I would meet him in the cloister, or kneel near him in choir, and I could not but see how close to God he was, and how mean and little and selfish I showed in comparison. Then I was ashamed of myself and of my desire to know everything, and for a while I was a little more humble.

After Matins on August 14th we assembled for Chapter and after the recommendations and accusations, the prior said that Father Hyacinth wished to speak to us. He crossed to where the old man was sitting and led him to his own stall, sitting himself in the nearest vacant one. I looked up and then lowered my eyes quickly. The old Father's face was so bright and shining that I could not bear to look at it.

He began to speak slowly and with many pauses and I knew that he was giving us his last testament. He said:

'Beloved brethren and dear children, the time has come for me to leave you, to go to the God who calls me. Do not grieve at this separation. Since Jesus Christ is our life, you will all find me again in him, and as I have loved you on earth, I shall love you still more in heaven. What St Dominic, our holy Father, left us as our inheritance, I in my turn am leaving you: the privations of poverty, the austerities of the Rule, the abnegation of obedience, the toils of the apostolate, mutual charity and, above all, the love and protection of Mary, our most tender Mother.'

He stopped, and one could hear by his labored breathing the effort that those last few words had cost him. Then, very slowly, he dragged himself to his feet and gave us his blessing. And I knew that it was the blessing of a saint. As he tottered down the chapter room leaning on the prior's arm, he muttered something about its being, for what it was worth, the blessing of an old man.

We saw no more of him for that day, but when at midnight we came into choir to sing Matins of the Assumption, Jasek was down before us, kneeling in his stall. Sung Mass followed Matins and the old Father went to Holy Communion, and by this we knew that he was not saying Mass that day.

When Mass was ended, there was a stir and bustle around, brothers hurrying backwards and forwards from the sacristy, and someone whispered that Father Jasek was going to be anointed. A chair was carried up to the front and the dying man came up, leaning on the prior's arm, and knelt at the altar rails. So Jasek was to receive Extreme Unction on his knees.

For a moment I felt angry and disgusted. It was almost like a show. It is usual for friars to be anointed lying on the bare ground; but this! Then, as I looked, for the first time there flashed through my mind some small understanding of the Pole, of his unbreakable spirit, his independence. For the second time Jasek was giving to God the offering of a free man; the first had been the voluntary dedication of his whole life and work, now he was giving life itself. God had made him free and, before God's altar, he was giving back the finished work; the free, complete and unstinted service of his freedom. And, in return, God was going to strengthen the free man for his last combat. This was no show, it was something genuine and magnificent.

He was anointed as he knelt there; only when it came to the feet, those feet which had travelled so far in search of souls, the prior helped him to sit down. Afterwards he made his Profession of Faith and renewed his Vows. Although I had only known him for such a short time, my mouth was dry and there was a big lump in my throat. Many of those around me, his brothers in all but blood, were openly crying. After all was over, the prior and the infirmarian almost carried him back to his cell. They say he lay there quite still in the most perfect peace.

Towards evening we were called to his bedside to say the prayers for the dying and to sing the *Salve*. Father Hyacinth lay there so calm, he was so fully conscious that it seemed to me that the old man would live sometime longer. But he himself knew better. As soon as the *Salve* was ended he began to speak; but not to us this time. He was saying the thirtieth psalm.

'*In te, Domine, speravi, non confundar in aeternum,*' he began, '*in justitia tua libera me. Inclina ad me aurem tuam, accelera ut eruas me. Esto mihi in Deum protectorem, et in domum refugii; ut salvum me facias. Quoniam fortitude mea et refugium meum es tu; et propter nomen tuum deduces me et enutrias me. Educes me de laqueo hoc, quam absconderunt mihi; quoniam tu es protector meus. In manus tuas commendo spiritum meum...*'

The voice died away, the breathing grew shallower, but the end was so easy that we could not tell the exact moment when he ceased to breathe. At last:

'*De profundis clamavi*,' said the prior, and we knew that Jasek had gone to God.

He died on August 15th, 1257, being seventy-two years of age and thirty-eight professed.

CHAPTER VII

How Kracow Honored Jasek

It was astonishing how quickly the news of Father Hyacinth's death found its way outside the priory. As soon as possible after washing and dressing it, the body was taken down to the church and placed in the Lady Chapel. This had hardly been done when the church was besieged by a throng of people of all sorts and conditions, come to pay their last reverence to one whom they had all loved and looked on as a saint.

There he lay at the feet of the statue he had brought from Kiev more than a decade of years before, to receive the homage of thousands. Four of the brothers kept watch day and night to prevent the habit being torn off him for relics. During the whole of that time people crowded the nave, moving slowly up until they had reached the place where the body lay. There they knelt, praying aloud and touching the dead man's hands and feet with kerchiefs they had brought. After a few minutes the brothers on guard moved them off down the aisle to make room for a fresh group.

Shortly after the church was opened to the public, I was kneeling there, praying a little and wondering more, when there was a stir and bustle in the porch, and ushers came in and began to make a way for someone of importance. The people near me crowded together and I heard them whisper: "The Bishop."

When a space had been cleared for him, the Lord John Prandotta, Bishop of Kracow, in full choir dress, appeared in the doorway. He had come in state with his chapter, as soon as he had learnt the news, to do honor to and to pray by the body of one who had been an intimate friend.

The day wore on and townsfolk began to give place to those who had come from farther afield. There were groups of friars from all the priories round, most of which had been founded by Jasek; there were nobles, citizens and peasants.

Late on the following day, I saw something which impressed me more than the Bishop with his canons, or the nobles In their almost barbaric splendor of dress. Again—this time after Vespers, for I could not tear myself away from the Lady Chapel—I was kneeling by the altar rail, when a door at the rear opened and a group of friars came in, headed by their huge, grizzled prior, Sadoc.

Sadoc had come to the east with Paul of Hungary. After working in Hungary for a number of years, he had been sent to Poland, to the novitiate house of Sandomierz to work under Hyacinth.

They had been friends, for friendships have always been a mark of our Order, and now the old prior had come to say 'Good-bye.' When he had heard of Jasek's illness, he had come at once, hoping to be in time to see him alive, but this was not to be. Sadoc's face was quite impassive and showed nothing of what he must have been feeling. This somehow made the little scene much more impressive. The great lion of a man knelt perfectly still beside the dead body of his friend for quite ten minutes; then he rose, gave one long deep sigh, raised the capuce with which, according to our custom, the face was covered, looked down in its shining radiance for half a moment, blessed the body and walked out through the door by which he had come. They say that he went straight into the choir and there he stayed.

That night we sang the Dirge, and next morning the Bishop pontificated and buried Jasek. Poles are musical people with beautiful voices and I have never before or since heard anything so impressive as that Mass. The funeral sermon preached by our prior was a surprise. I had expected something flowery and emotional; this was awe-inspiring in its terse simplicity.

'Hyacinth our father and our brother, received the habit from the hands of our Father Dominic himself. Once professed he was sent to Kracow to introduce there the newly founded Order of Friars Preachers.

'No one was more humble and modest than he, and I believe that throughout his life he preserved his virginity untarnished. In order to keep the flesh subject to the spirit, each night he disciplined himself to blood. His self control in the matters of food and drink was wonderful; very frequently he fasted on bread and water. He often spent whole nights prostrate in prayer in the church, and when sometimes he was obliged to rest his weary body, he slept either lying on the ground, or leaning against the altar.

'When he was not praying he spent his time in studying, giving instructions, preaching or hearing Confessions. It is difficult to enumerate the number of countries, differing widely in manners and customs, through which he journeyed preaching the Gospel. He was unwearied in his work for God; nor is it possible to tell how many heathen he converted, or how many bad Christians he brought to repentance...'

These few plain words did me good, for they meant far more to me than whole volumes of miracles. I could not work wonders as Father Jasek did, but from my distance I could at least follow him in his life of prayer, work and preaching, and penance.

Hyacinth Odrowatz, the apostle of Poland, was buried in the church of the Holy Trinity, built for the friars by Bishop Ivo his uncle and the citizens of Kracow. Between '43 and '45, the city had been captured by the Tartars in their great march of conquest westward. The Poles were the defenders of Christian Europe against Asia; but one heard little of it, for they did not boast. The church and priory being of stone, were not destroyed by the barbarians, and after the wave had fallen back on Asia again, the town had been rebuilt and all was so completely restored that it was difficult to believe it had ever been destroyed.

An hour or so after the Funeral we had an unexpected summons to the chapter room, where we found the Bishop with his college of canons and a number of other priests and layfolk. When we had assembled, the prior told us briefly that the Bishop wished to speak to us about Father Hyacinth.

The Bishop stood up, settled his robes nervously and began to talk. It was not easy to follow him for he seemed so dazed that he found coherent speech a difficulty. However, I managed to gather the gist of what he was saying.

'As I was returning to the cathedral after burying my beloved friend, Father Jasek, I think that God vouchsafed to show me something of the glory of his servant. I was, as it were, carried out of myself, and was watching a procession of figures clothed in white, which was defiling past me. Following these came two majestic figures shining with special glory; one was a bishop in full pontificals, and the other a Friar Preacher, one of yourselves. On his head there were two magnificent crowns.

'The bishop turned to me and said: "I am Stanislaus, your predecessor in the See of Kracow. The man beside me is Hyacinth of the Order of Preachers. You see that he is wearing a double crown; that of a Doctor and that of a Virgin. I have been sent to lead him to his throne of glory."

'After saying this, he intoned the Antiphon: "*Lux perpetua lucebit sanctis tuis, Domine.*" And the angels took up the chant: "*Et aeternitas temporum, Alleluia, Alleluia, Alleluia.*" Whilst they sang this, they were gradually drawn up into a cloud of overwhelming brightness.'

The Bishop's voice died into silence; to say more was evidently beyond him. We also were struck dumb and motionless; borne down as it were and crushed by the greatness of what we had heard. For Hyacinth was our brother.

Then, quite suddenly, the cantor broke into the *Te Deum*. The tension snapped, and we shouted the hymn until the chapter room seemed to rock with the volume of sound.

After that we filed out into the cloister, but for a long time no one could speak of what had happened.

CHAPTER VIII

Concerning Father Ceslas and the Lady Zedislava

Quite a number of those who had come for the funeral stayed on for a few days in the guest quarters. Among them was a young man whose appearance took my fancy. He had happened to be in the neighborhood when the news of Father Jasek's death reached him and he had come at once since he had known the Father well. His name was Stanislaw of Jablonia; his father was Gallo of Lemburg of the family of Markvast, who owned a castle near Jablonia in Bohemia. The young man's mother had been a close friend of Father Ceslas at Breslau, and she had erected a priory for him at Gabel, or Jablona, a small town on the frontiers of Bohemia and Poland where her husband had built a castle.

The day after the funeral I happened to be passing along the cloister when I met young Stanislaw in company with one of the friars. They stopped and the father introduced us.

'Here,' he said, 'is Thomas of England, who has been sent here to study foreign manners and customs. As is natural, he is specially interested in anything Dominican. Your mother was so closely connected with the Order that I am sure he will like to talk to you.'

He winked at me as he said this, and I knew that he had other work on hand and wished to turn the young man over to me. I, for my part, was quite pleased, for a Bohemian should be more German than Polish, and by this time I was becoming interested in types.

We turned out into the cloister garden and, after answering a few questions that he put to me about England, I asked him whether he had known Father Hyacinth's relative, Ceslas.

'He was a close friend of my family,' he replied, 'but as I was only a child when he died, I knew Father Jasek better. My parents, of course, knew both of them well. Father Ceslas gave my mother the habit of the Third Order. She died three years ago, having outlived him twelve years.'

'Is your father still alive?'

'Yes. He's an old man now. A good father and, taking it all in all, an indulgent husband to my mother, who was very holy, but perhaps a little odd.'

'Holy people are very often a little odd,' I remarked.

Stanislaw threw back his head and laughed. 'That is true,' he answered. 'But you must not think that I am disparaging my mother in any way. She was a wonderful wife and a wonderful mother; only sometimes my father must have found her doings a little trying.'

'For instance?' I asked.

The young man laughed again. 'For instance,' he repeated. 'Well, you must know that my mother was in

Prague, about seventy or eighty miles from Jablonia, when Hyacinth and Ceslas passed through on their way to Poland. In fact they made quite a long stay, and Hyacinth left Ceslas in charge of the priory there. My mother was captivated by the Friars Preachers and their life, and nothing would satisfy her when she returned home but to have a church and priory built for them at Gabel, called in our language Jablona, where my father had one of his residences. Now—and this is what I mean by oddness—not content with giving orders, she must needs take a share in the work. So she used to go out at night and carry stones from the quarry to the site of the convent; not of much practical use, and very annoying to my father, who really put up with it very patiently.'

'Was the priory finished?'

'Indeed it was, and Zedislava, my mother, invited Father Hyacinth to come and take possession. He was not able to come, so he sent Father Ceslas in his place. It was before he left Gabel that he gave my mother the Habit. After all that is the only really odd thing that she did. Her penances were terrible, but we knew nothing of these until after her death, when we found her hair shirt and some much used disciplines.'

He paused for a minute and then added: 'The friars from her priory of St Lawrence in Gabel were with her when she died, and she was quite conscious and praying to the end. Her life was one long prayer and more than once I have seen her quite out of herself. But all the same, she never neglected either her family or her household. So perhaps, after all, her small oddities were a very trifling matter.'

'Can you tell me anything about Father Ceslas?'

'Oh, Father Ceslas was a very great man. When he came to Prague, I have heard my mother say, the Pope had just mediated in a quarrel between King Premislas and Archbishop Andrew. Ceslas captivated the pair of them, and it was a matter of which could do most to honor the Friars Preachers. Between them they built a large priory and when that was finished they built a convent for nuns as well. After that Father Ceslas left prior Henry of Moravia to take his place and went on to Breslau. Breslau is north west of Jablonia, and not so far as Prague which is to the south east.'

'Did he remain at Breslau?'

'He built the priory and church of St Adelbert and made that his headquarters; but he was much away, for he travelled in Poland, Bohemia, Moravia, Saxony, Ruthenia, and the countries bordering on the Elbe and the Baltic sea. He worked almost as many miracles as his brother, and the finest of them was at Breslau not long before he died. Do you know about the Tartar invasion?'

'Not a great deal I'm afraid.'

'If you are studying our manners and customs, it will pay you to find out all you can about the Tartars, for they have had an enormous share in making the history of the countries around here. Between '42 and '45 there was a great invasion—an organized invasion for conquest and not merely a raid. They simply swarmed over Poland and Hungary; and the countries to the west of them too had their share of trouble.'

'I will certainly take your advice and learn what I can about the Tartars, but in the meantime tell me about Father Ceslas, please.'

'It was in '42 that the Tartars besieged Breslau and Ceslas was there at the time. The city consisted of large suburbs and in the centre was a citadel very strongly fortified. A year before the Father had prophesied the siege of the city. This was before the Tartars ravaged Hungary and Bulgaria. Now they killed the King of Poland who tried to stop them and prepared to lay siege to Breslau.

'Knowing what to expect from such an enemy, the people from all the country round set fire to their houses and crops, and fled to the city. The Tartars, finding all the land laid waste, concluded that the same thing would have happened in Breslau. But Duke Henry, the commander of the garrison, was not that sort of man. He ordered the citizens to bring all their food stuffs into the citadel and prepare to stand a siege. Your priory was inside the walls.

'When the Tartars reached Breslau, prepared to loot the city without more ado, they were exceedingly angry to find that their job was not so easy as they expected. But they had no intention of giving up their project and so they brought up their troops, their scaling ladders and the rest and invested the stronghold. Things were not made any easier for them by the suburbs having been laid waste, so that they had little or no cover.

'The Governor had his own anxieties, for there were many more people inside the walls than he had reckoned on, and he knew it could not be long before they were starved out. By the end of the third day things were looking very black indeed, when he bethought himself of asking for the prayers of the friars, and particularly of Ceslas.

'Father Ceslas spent the night in prayer and in the morning went out on the ramparts and stood looking out on the enemy. A cousin of mine who was there told me that they were preparing for assault and were scurrying around like an ants' nest when someone has disturbed it. Their horses were tethered in the rear of the army and they were bringing up ladders and there were hordes of them, each with his javelin, waiting for the order of assault. It was an ordered army and very well disciplined and commanded.

'Suddenly, the sky was heavily overcast and grew as black as night. Then the whole was lighted by sheet after sheet of flame. My cousin ran to the nearest watch tower for shelter, but Ceslas remained where he was. My cousin could see him through an arrow slit. He was standing on a bastion not far from a turret, as calm as though nothing whatever was happening. Fire was playing all up and down him and there seemed to be a great ball of flame over his head, which was covered with his capuce. The noise I am told was frightful, and above it all sounded the shrieks of wounded and dying men.

'In about quarter of an hour everything cleared and the sun came out again. The Governor and his captains were on the ramparts looking down, and at the foot of the wall lay hundreds of dead Tartars, while hundreds more lay wounded. The wounded men and the few left unhurt were shouting for the friars to come out and baptize them. Far in the distance, our men could see the remainder of that great army, fleeing away as fast as their horses could carry them.

'The Governor ordered everyone to go to the cathedral to sing the *Te Deum* and then the gates were opened. The friars were kept busy for days after, instructing and baptizing.'

In company with a Bohemian this time, I found myself back in the realm of fantasy. If such wonders did happen how was it they never happened in England? Pulling myself together I thanked Stanislaw for his take and asked him what else happened to Father Ceslas.

'Father Ceslas died not long after. I had the story of his death from a friar who was there. He called the community of St Adelbert together and said to them: "Put your confidence in the merits of Jesus Christ and in the protection of his Virgin Mother. Remember that you cannot be perfect Religious without being first perfect Christians. Monastic observances are good and holy on in so far as they are based on humility and self-renunciation."'

There was similarity of thought between the cousins. I myself had heard Father Hyacinth say much the same.

'Did he say anything else?' I asked.

'They say his last words were: "Lord, I have no other desire but thee; deign in return to admit me to your divine company."'

At this minute a brother came up to me: 'Father Provincial wishes to see you,' he said.

I hurried off to the provincial's room. He was looking at me with the same half amused, wholly enigmatic smile that I had seen on his face when he read my letters of credential.

'You know that Prague is in the Polish Province.' He said. 'Brother Albert is going to lecture in our studium there for the winter session. You are to go with him, to study under him. Later, in the spring, when he returns here, I have told him to find an escort to take you to Hungary. You should have some knowledge of the Tartars; and Hungary is the best place for you to study their manner of life and their doings. After a year there, you will come back to Kracow as occasion offers. Then, if you are ready, you shall return to England.'

I made the *Venia*. But I was not looking forward to my new obedience any more than I had to the one which sent me to Poland. It would certainly be useful for me to go to Hungary to study the Tartars; but I had taken my degree and been Lector for a term at Oxford, and I did not relish beginning as a scholar again in a foreign school, just as if I were no more than a student or a novice.

There was one bright spot, however, in the fact that I was to go with Brother Albert; and both as student and companion I was glad to be with him. Perhaps, even, this new obedience might prove as profitable as the one given me in England. I had no idea then how useful my contact with Albert was to prove to me.

I went out into the cloister to find him.

CHAPTER IX

I Go To Prague With Brother Albert

At the end of August, Brother Albert and I took our staves and knapsacks and set out westward for Prague. We made the journey on foot for the most part, with occasional lifts in farm carts; or we travelled for short spells by boat, when we chanced on a river flowing in the direction we were taking.

It was not long before we left the Polish plains and began to make our way through the Bohemian forest. If I had found Poland flatter than any country I had ever seen, now for the first time in my life I was to meet with real mountains. We took a route through the passes between them as far as we were able, but sometimes we had to climb; past beeches and oaks, through pines with their crisp carpet of needles and their acrid, tonic scent, out on the bare rocks, from where we looked down on a tumbled world of hill and forest around and below us. And the air was like wine.

At other times we made our way through rocky defiles with the green forest world all about us; or again pushed our way through the woods themselves. Sometimes we followed the course of a river or stream, which opened out on to brief plains, dotted with wooden villages, where the sound of the woodman's axe made unending music. I would not have missed that journey for the world; a perfect journey with a perfect companion, for what Albert did not know about country life was not worth knowing.

It was after we had been travelling for the best part of a week that one evening, after we had supped on bread and goats' milk, given us by the housewife in a lonely mountain cottage, and were sitting out under the pines, with the stars blazing overhead, I broached a subject which had occupied much of my thought.

'Albert,' I began, 'you know what a man Jasek was; how great and how simple?' Albert nodded. 'I can't tell you how much I love and revere him. What an example he is to me. But, some of those miracles, you know. All that river-walking, for instance?'

I laughed as I said it to hide my embarrassment; but Albert did not laugh. He just nodded his head again.

'I quite understand,' he said, 'and I am going to do my best to answer you as I think Master Albert would have done. You know that I studied under those two great Masters, Albert of Cologne and Thomas Aquinas? It was at the new Generale in Cologne, from '48, when they came from Paris, to '54, when I was sent here to lecture in my turn. Master Albert was Regent of Studies and Master Thomas Master of Students. If you had asked either of them, I think they would have said that, after you had taken miracle in the Universal and generalized, then you must distinguish miracle from miracle in the singular and concrete.' He stopped.

'Please go on,' I said. I had heard of the fame of Master Albert and Master Thomas and I was certain that I should be given a sufficient reason for all I was told.

'Well,' began Albert again, 'in the first place, speaking in the Universal, miracles—per se—are facts. You agree to that don't you?' I nodded in my turn.

'I think that you will also agree that a miracle is something which transcends the Laws of Nature and therefore is directly referable to the Author of Nature, who, because he is their author, can abrogate them when it pleases him?' Again I nodded.

'I think you will further agree that in many cases the Author of Nature abrogates his own laws in favor of someone, because the miracle worker possesses faith and love of God in a super eminent degree? In the Universal, then, miracles are. But in the Particular, I distinguish miracle from miracle and judge each on its own merits.

'To come to the Particular, in the case of Jasek. The man of God, drawn by intense love of God and souls, was given mastery over such things as water, because he was raised above them and given dominion over them in particular instances, by reason of this intense love of God. Even in the natural order we speak of such things as an overmastering desire or fear; which means that a person, carried out of himself by such passions as desire or fear, is able to do things which ordinarily are not possible to him. A man chased by a wild beast will leap chasms which he could not do without that incentive. A hunter, engaged in following a stag, pushes through thickets, impervious to wounds and bruises which would normally cause him consciousness of pain. If such phenomena are found in the order of nature, still more will they be found in the supernatural order.

'I think that Father Ceslas expresses something of this idea when, being obliged to cross a river on missionary work, he is reported to have said to himself: "When our Savior went in search of sinners he saw the sea become solid under his feet. As for you, although you are his unworthy servant, you are of the number of those to whom he has bequeathed his power over the elements. If you only have faith these rough waves will not stop you." To a dead child he said: "In the Name of him who gives his word of power to preachers of the Gospel, arise!" And the child who had been drowned and in the water for eight days, stood up at once. Intense faith. Intense trust.

'In the Gospel of St Mark Chapter XIV verses 15 to 18, we read: "And he said to them: Go ye into the whole world and preach the Gospel to every creature. He that believeth and is baptized shall be saved; and he that believeth not shall be condemned. And these signs shall follow them that believe. In my name they shall cast out devils. They shall speak with new tongues. They shall take up serpents; and if they shall drink any deadly thing it shall not hurt them. They shall lay their hands on the sick and they shall recover." Our Lord's promise.'

There was silence while Albert regained his breath and I tried to assimilate what he had said. But not yet satisfied I began again:

'Yes, Albert, I grant all this. But some of those miracles, and those journeys?' Then I blurted out what I had found most unpalatable: 'When Jasek chased the devil over the river, for instance.'

Albert threw back his head and laughed: 'Thomas, where is your logic?' he cried, 'it is bad reasoning to generalize from particulars. Surely you realize that we are not expected to swallow wholesale every miracle presented to us? And as for the journeys, Jasek was of course a great missionary and traveler, and a legend of his travels has grown up around him. Each teller has added a little. Look in our chronicle, when you go back, and you will find sober fact, more wonderful than what you have heard, and much easier to believe.'

I laughed too: 'A good deal has stuck in my throat unswallowed.'

Albert sat quiet for a minute: 'I think that the Master would say that a legend grows up around each wonder-worker, for the credulous cannot distinguish the natural from the preternatural, and are only too ready to cry out: "A miracle" without first examining evidence.'

'Then the young friars at Kracow were telling me tall stories. They didn't believe themselves what they were telling me so seriously? I wondered at the time, but they looked so solemn.' I was aghast; this was turning the tables on me with a vengeance, for I had considered myself the sophisticated person.

'Quite possibly,' replied Albert. 'Neither you nor I are Poles, so I can say it without offence; they are not always easy to fathom. They may have thought that you were giving yourself airs and so treated you accordingly. You have rather a superior way with you, which I should imagine you are utterly unconscious of, as though you knew more than most. To return to the miracle which was one of those you could not swallow, here is a possible explanation.

'The secret worship of an idol is interfering with the success of Jasek's preaching and, being a practical person, he sets out to destroy it. There is a thin coating of ice on the river, sufficient to support a light weight, and so Jasek crosses on foot. Some peasants watch him crossing and, being at too great a distance to see the ice, conclude without further examination that he is "river-walking," a miracle. Mind you, I make no definite assertion that it is not, but, for myself, I cannot see that there is sufficient reason to call for a genuine miracle in what he has set out to do.

'Jasek destroys his idol and is going back the way he has come when the priest of the grove discovers what has happened to his precious statue and comes after him with a club. Jasek realizes that the priest is a heavy man who will probably go through the ice; so he chases him back with his staff, shouting that it is dangerous for him to trust himself on the ice. The peasants cannot hear Jasek as he has his back to them. They can't hear the priest and imagine the words he is saying. And so, behold Jasek driving off the devil!'

Albert paused and turned such a comical look on me that I laughed until the tears ran down my cheeks. It was so delightfully commonplace and such a sane explanation; and I had made such a fool of myself. When I had recovered some measure of gravity he took up his theme.

'Now, it is of faith that God answers our prayers, but he does not always answer them in the way we expect, and he certainly does not always suspend the Laws of Nature to answer them. I think there is an example of what I mean in what is called "Ceslas's Miracle" in saving Breslau from the Tartars. I am not asserting that it is not a miracle, any more than I did about the idol; I am only suggesting a possible natural explanation.

'Father Ceslas prayed God to save Breslau and he did save it. Ceslas was praying on the battlements and he saw it saved. By the way, you know the story don't you?' I nodded.

'As you know it was saved by fire. His prayers were answered, but it may be that the fire which destroyed many of the Tartars and put the remainder to flight was caused by a severe but perfectly natural thunderstorm, sent by God for the purpose.

'Now lightning has an affinity to iron and steel, and the Tartars were carrying scaling ladders and steel-tipped lances. Wool has a repelling force on lightning. Ceslas had on a woolen habit and cappa and he had drawn his woolen capuce over his head. He had no idea, of course of protecting himself; he was dressed for prayer in choir dress.

'Now, you can see what may have happened. The steel drew the lightning to the Tartars and they themselves afforded a path by which it could run to earth. The wool protected Ceslas. The lightning played around and over him, but it did not strike. So you see, people watching him apparently surrounded by fire but unhurt by it, not recognizing cause and effect, cried out "A miracle." And I am sure that Ceslas himself would have no idea as to what he owed his safety.'

'Oh!' was all the answer I could find to make to this wonderful explanation, but Albert seemed to find it sufficient.

'It is time to sleep,' he remarked crisply and, wrapping himself in his cappa, he stretched himself on a bed of pine needles.

I did the same, and lay for a long time looking up at the glowing stars. I had not felt so lighthearted since the day when I had met the sailor on Thames bank and my adventures had begun. I had heard at Oxford something of my companion's two Masters, of their new method of exposition and of Master Albert's knowledge of natural science. If the Brother Albert beside me was a worthy disciple, as he gave every promise of being, it would be a fine thing for me simply to go to school again when I reached Prague and study with the novices the new learning he had brought from Cologne. There would be no Studium Generale for me it was true; but I could pick up much learning in the studium at Prague.

'*Dirupisti vincula mea,** said I over and over again until at last I fell asleep.

---

* You have broken my chains.

CHAPTER X

How I Wintered in Prague

Prague is a magnificent city, built on both banks of the river Moldau, and the foundations of its cathedral of St Vitus were laid more than three centuries ago. But you can learn all about Prague from any traveler who has been in the east, and so I will go on to what concerned me much more intimately, something that you can learn from no one else.

Our convent of St Clement was as fine as any I have seen; it was built for Father Ceslas in 1222 on the left bank of the river. It can house a hundred friars and stands quite near to the royal palace. It was built by King Premislas, who gave Ceslas many rich gifts for the church. I have seen the twenty-four chalices and the silver crucifix which were among his presents.

The Knights Templars are very powerful in the city, as in the whole of Bohemia which they have erected into a separate priory. There are many convents and monasteries beside our own, among them that of the

71

Poor Clares, dedicated to St Agnes, and built by a royal princess of the same name, who is now its prioress.

But as far as I was concerned the interest of that winter centered in the lectures given by Brother Albert; and very often I did not leave the precincts for days at a time. There were not more than seven or eight students in the class. These were the pick of the novitiate and were to go on later to Cologne, Bologna and Paris, as there was then no university or studium generale in Prague.

Every morning we assembled in the hall on benches round the Master's chair, wrapped our feet in straw as protection against the biting cold, listened intently to Brother Albert's exposition and assimilated it as far as we were able. These morning lectures were always on Philosophy or Theology. In the afternoons we had repetitions, either among ourselves, or with a lector. In the evenings we learnt something of natural science. This proceeding and the matter of the lectures were familiar to me, but not their mode of presentation, and it was not long before I found that I was learning so much that I determined to say nothing about the lectorate I had gained at Oxford, and to study as a simple student.

Brother Albert lectured according to the method of Master Albert and Master Thomas. I had never before realized that science could be at the same time so profound and yet so crystal clear. Master Thomas has since written a Sum of his teaching in Theology, which is now within the reach of all. In those days there was no written word and Brother Albert taught us by word of mouth only, as he had been taught. No Sum, however perfect, can give any idea of the richness of the living word spoken by one who had learnt from the Masters themselves. Brother Albert did more, he fired us with his own enthusiasm for the teachers themselves as well as for their teaching,

Even after these thirty years, I carry in my old mind one vivid recollection of how the teaching of Master Thomas was food for both mind and soul.

It was Lent, if I remember rightly, and I had been thinking of Brother Kazemierz and Sandomierz and the great terrible crucifix at the foot of the church tower. In Theology we had been studying the life of Christ, and the day's lecture had been on the Crucifixion. Brother Albert had given seven reasons why, according to Master Thomas, crucifixion was the most fitting death for Our Lord.

'In the first place,' he told us, 'as Christ is our exemplar, he was showing us that no death is to be feared. Death as it is, per se, is not feared by many people, but most people have a fear of some particular kind of death. By dying the most dreadful death of all, Christ showed us that we need fear no kind of death since we are following him.

'In the second place he died in the open to consecrate by his death both heaven and earth.

'He died with arms wide stretched to embrace both Jews and Gentiles.

'He died with upraised head, pointing to heaven, our goal.

'His head raised on high signifies the aim of our good works, the outstretched arms its breadth and scope, the feet that our good works must rest on God, the cross buried deep that grace must be their foundation.

'He died on wood that he might be the fruit of the Tree of Life, since, by eating the forbidden fruit, Adam brought death.

'Finally, he died in fulfillment of all prophecies.'

Turning these reasons over in my mind, with the picture of the Sandomierz crucifix before my imagination, I had dimly seen a glimmer of something far beyond anything I had ever conceived. I tried to clarify this conception of mine and give it some foundation of reason, so that I might return to and study it whenever I wanted; but it somehow escaped me, and remained as formless as a cloud on a bright surface.

Sometimes Albert would invite me to go out with him; and then our talk always turned on his two beloved Masters. He said that physically Thomas was a huge man, with a mighty mind, far greater even than that of his master, Albert; but he was also a man of the most profound and unfeigned humility. In illustration of this, he once told me a story of Thomas's student days.

It appears that he is a very silent man. His fellow students, noticing this, thought him stupid and, out of kindness of heart, offered to repeat the lessons over for him afterwards. Thomas accepted gratefully and gave no sign that he had already grasped what his instructors were explaining to him. It happened, however, one day that one of his fellow students made a mistake in what he was saying, giving a wrong conclusion to a piece of reasoning. Then Thomas's love of truth prevailed over his humility and he said: 'Dear Brother, the Master did not say that; he said—' and repeated the whole train of reasoning word for word.

After this, the amazed novices changed their tactics, and it was they who asked their former pupil to give them the repetition. Eventually this reached the ears of the Master of Students, and one day he hid himself in the hall, to hear Thomas give a clearer, more brilliant exposition than Albert himself. He went to the Regent. 'The man we call the dumb ox has such knowledge that it is a wonder even to hear him. If I had not heard him myself I should not have believed his powers.' When Master Albert heard this he was overjoyed, for he had always known that Thomas had a mighty intellect.

In the evenings, as I have already said, the lectures were on physical science, geography and the like. In this branch of knowledge Master Albert was supreme. Our Albert told us that the Master was wont to say: '*Experimentum solum certificate tallibus.*' So, among many other experiments, he had made a winter garden where, all the year round, he grew summer fruit and flowers. Albert said that on the feast of the Epiphany eight years previously, the Master had shown William of Holland, the King of the Romans, plants and fruit trees in full blossom. He had been using glass to concentrate the sun's rays and refraction to direct them where he wanted.

On more than one night Albert took us out-of-doors to show us the heavens. He explained that the figures seen on the moon's surface were not, as has hitherto been believed, the reflection of the seas and mountains of the earth, but her own configuration. He spoke of planets and fixed stars, and pointing to the Milky Way, said that it was simply a vast assemblage of stars.

At other times he spoke of the shape of the earth and of its five zones. He told us of the two polar regions, and said that animals living there had thick coats and that these were most probably white in color. When asked the reason for his theory, he explained that in snow covered countries, white would serve as a protection, just as the dun coats of our wolves and bears mingled with the pied shadows of the forests.

These are only fragments which my old memory retains of a rich store of knowledge; poor shades of what was once a living reality.

I could have visited Breslau and Jablona if I had cared to do so, but I did not think I should be disobeying my superiors by staying where I was and learning with the novices. Even at home I heard quite a deal about Father Ceslas and the Lady Zedislava; and this was interesting since I now saw the lady from a different angle to that given me by Stanislaw her son.

I heard of her early life, of her strict upbringing in her father's castle of Krisanov in Moravia on the road from Saar to Brunn. Her mother Sibylle, was the daughter of the Count Palatine of Witelsbach, and had come to Bohemia in the train of Cunegunde, the daughter of the Emperor Philip of Hohenstaufen, when she married Wenceslas, heir to the throne of Bohemia. At the age of seven Zedislava had run away to be a hermit; but when she understood the pain she had caused her mother, she promised that for the future her parents' will should be her law, and this promise she faithfully kept.

Her husband Gallo of Jablona was a soldier who had gained distinction by his devotion to the Kings Ottokar and Wenceslas. The friars did not seem to consider him an indulgent husband. They said he was rough and fierce;

76

but that Zedislava's gentleness had tamed him. They spoke of her penances and how she regulated these. When her husband was away she fasted and took severe disciplines, but when he was at home she contented herself with slipping out of bed to pray when she saw him asleep.

I heard another side of her exploits as a builder. I was told that the priory at Jablona owed its strength and beauty to the enthusiasm with which she had inspired the workmen by herself helping at night with the roughest and most laborious part of the work. Perhaps her actual stone carrying feats did not come up to that of men brought up to the work; but she shamed them into working harder than they had ever done in their lives. In fact all spoke of her as a saint.

For the rest, our life was passed in the same fashion as we live it in all our major priories such as Oxford and London, so that I was at home; but you would only find my describing it as a wearisome repetition of something you already know at first hand.

The winter passed all too quickly and, with the spring, Albert had to go back to Kracow and I was due to go on to Pesth. One of the friars from Prague was going as far as Esztergom and I was to go with him.

Albert was leaving the day after our boat was to sail.

When I said goodbye and tried to thank him for all he had done for me both mentally and spiritually, I found myself completely tongue-tied. But he seemed to understand all that I wanted to say, told me to say no more about it, for I had been a help to him also. The wharf from which we were to leave was at the gateway of the priory, and he came down to wish me 'God speed' with a gay promise of our meeting again in Kracow in the following year.

As we went downstream, my last glimpse of him was standing in the gateway and waving his hand.

CHAPTER XI

How I Went to Hungary

As I have already said, I was travelling with a friar who had business in Esztergom; there I was to leave him and go to Pesth on foot. The road journey, though more tiring, was also somewhat more direct, as by taking to my feet I avoided a bend in the river. As we passed out of sight of the priory, I looked back and waved to Albert, still standing near the wharf. I hoped I should meet him again when I returned in the following year.

Father Nicholas, my companion, was an elderly man, and never have I met one with less to say for himself. During the first day I tried to engage him in conversation and received nothing but mono-syllables in reply. So, after that, I gave it up as a bad job and contented myself with following him wherever he went, obeying his directions and, for the rest, saying no more than was necessary.

We journeyed practically the whole distance by boat, only walking from one river to another as necessity arose. A considerable part of our way took us through mountainous country, and I rejoiced just to sit in the bows of the boat, drinking in the clear air and feasting my eyes on the hills round; or, when the river chanced to cut its way between two hills, gazing up the rocky sides of the pass, and glimpsing the narrow thread of sky atop. Part of my childhood was spent in the Peak country, and hills are almost living creatures to me.

I suppose that these same hills must have stirred memory, for seldom, since I became a Friar Preacher, have I looked back over the past; my turning has naturally been to what is to come, what the future holds in store. But, one moonlit night, sitting in the bows of the boat, my memory found its way back to my childhood.

I had been thinking, as I often did, of Jasek and of his story of our Father Dominic's miracle in raising to life the young Napoleon, and of his own call to be a friar. God has his way with each one of us and, since he is infinite in resource, the experience of each one is unique.

My father was a master weaver in Leicester. The town is an exceedingly ancient one, and the country round famous for its sheep. My father married twice; by his first wife he had seven children, of whom I was the youngest. My mother dying when I was about a year old, my father married again, and by his second wife had eight children.

My step-mother was very kind to me and treated me as if I had been one of her own little ones, but from babyhood, the oily smell of fleece in the workshop, which pervaded the whole house, made me sick and so I was never well in Leicester.

When I was about eight years old, my mother's father came to the city on business and, as was natural, he stayed at our house. Noticing what a puny sickly child I was, he offered to take me back with him. As by this time my step-mother had a houseful of babes of her own, the offer was gratefully accepted and I was taken back to my mother's old home, an ancient house near Chapel in le Frith, which had belonged to my grandfather's Saxon forefathers time out of mind.

It was not long before I became a strong healthy lad living as I did a carefree life, helping on the farm, climbing the hills, fishing in the streams and, as I grew older, going on most mornings in the week to the village priest, a learned, kindly old man, who taught me to read, write and compute; later Latin and a little Greek were added to the list.

I got into mischief like any other lad, and many a beating did I get for poaching, game stealing and night fishing. My bedroom, a tiny corner under the thatch, for I did not sleep with the men in the hall, had a small window, and often, after being sent to rest at sundown, when the moon was high, I clambered out and spent a night on the hills. I used to watch the sunrise and then sneak back to my pallet. My grandfather thought I was a sad slug-a-bed. He little knew.

Occasionally I paid my father a visit, finding the fleece no more palatable as I grew older, but for the most part my life was spent uneventfully in Chapel in le Frith until, soon after my sixteenth birthday, news was brought by a pedlar that my step-mother had recently died. My grandfather and I talked things over. He was now an old man and was thinking of turning the farm over to my eldest uncle, a married man with a large family. He told me he considered it my duty to visit my father, and stay to help him if I was needed and could stomach the fleece. So I went down to Leicester, riding a cob which my grandfather had given me for my birthday and feeling mighty proud of myself.

My father was very glad to see me and, as my brothers had already set up on their own and my stepmother's eldest children were girls, it seemed to me that I might be of use to him. A chance meeting was to change my life, just as it did on Thames bank seven years later.

I was crossing the market place one day when I saw a crowd round the cross. I went up to see what was happening and found a man in white with a black cloak and hood, standing on the steps and preaching. He was very much in earnest and I stayed to listen, first out of simple curiosity, but later because I was fascinated both by the preacher and by what he was saying. He was speaking about the Passion of Christ and was making it so real and lively that I could not tear myself away.

In an undertone, I asked the man next me who the preacher was and I was told that he was a Blackfriar of the Order of Preachers. I had heard something of these and their work so I studied him more closely.

Then, without any willing on my part, something happened in me, something in my soul, a stirring which was quite independent of the preacher or his words. I heard, as it were, a voice within me saying: 'Come, follow me,' and I felt at the same time a powerful drawing to join the preacher and to become one as he was.

God's call is a most strange and wonderful thing. It is so entirely apart from any willing of one's own and so inexplicable to those who have not heard the call. People may desire the religious life, or their parents may desire it for them, and there may be all manner of good reasons for their becoming monks or nuns, but unless God himself says 'Come,' there is no real vocation and what is for us a joyous life will be for them nothing but weariness and monotony. Monks in monasteries without a true vocation are at the root of relaxation.

The impulse to become a Preacher myself was so strong that, as soon as the sermon was ended, I went up to the friar.

'Will you take me with you?' I asked.

He smiled at me in a friendly way. 'What makes you ask that?' he asked.

'I want to be a Friar Preacher,' I answered.

'For how long have you wanted this?' he asked again.

Then I felt myself flush up, being no more than a lad and shy, and feeling that I should be laughed at, which no lad likes. But I answered truly: 'For the matter of half an hour or so.'

He threw back his head and laughed at that. But seeing that I was in earnest and a little hurt at his laughter, he added quite seriously: 'The Spirit of God breatheth where he will. The call of God comes to each of us in a different way. This may be your call. If you are still of the same mind this evening, come up to our priory.'

I went straight back to my father's house and the— what for want of a better word I will call—compulsion was stronger than ever on me. My father was in the workshop and I called him out and told him of the preaching friar and of how I felt I must become one of the Order of Friars Preachers.

And he, in his turn, asked me why, and for the life of me I could not tell him, only that I knew I had to go. So he blessed me and bade me 'God speed,' for he had always wanted one of his sons to be a priest, and why not a Friar Preacher as well as any other? But at the back of my mind I had a thought that perhaps he was not altogether sorry it should be me; having lived so little at home and being of so little use as a weaver.

And I went up to the priory, as I had been told, that very afternoon, all in a daze, only sure that I was doing right; and the prior clothed me the same evening in the chapter room, and I have never since looked back.

There was the novitiate, study, Oxford and London, and then this chase across Europe following my obedience to study humanity. Some things, most things, I have loved; some things, a few things, I have hated, but I have never wanted to change; I have never regretted what I have done and—I have never been weary of my life.

I had begun to reach the place where past and present and future mingle in one tangle past sorting, when I heard a movement and saw Father Nicholas looking over at me from the place farther astern where he had been nodding.

'*In pace et in idipsum, dormiam et requiescam,*' said he and for the first time since we began our journey I caught the varies twilight of a smile on his lips. Taciturn and phlegmatic as Father Nicholas was, he was not weary of his life any more than I was.

'You had better lie down and rest too,' he added. 'We've quite a long tramp tomorrow.'

I settled myself on the deck floor under the seat and wrapped my cappa round me.

Two days later the boat tied up at a wharf in Esztergom; Father Nicholas set off for the priory but, as I had the chance of a companion, a travelling pedlar, to set me on my right way, I said goodbye to him on the wharf and started off at once for Pesth. I was certain to find other opportunities of visiting Esztergom.

CHAPTER XII

How I Travelled to Buda

The distance from Esztergom to Buda, as the crow flies, is as near as I can guess from seventy to eighty miles. At least I know that we left the wharf at noon and my companion said that he hoped to reach the journey's end in from three to four days. Hungary, like Poland, is a plain but, instead of merging into other countries without a break, the former is bounded by hilly country on the north, north-east and north-west. These mountains serve, to some extent, as a barrier between the kingdom and the barbarians of Asia. I thought the land very fertile; for I saw great stretches of corn growing and large grazing grounds for sheep and cattle. The region through which we were travelling seemed well populated, for it was dotted over with villages of rather strange looking wooden houses.

My companion could speak the lingua franca and, as during my year in Poland I had learnt to understand and speak the language with reasonable fluency, we were able to talk together and I learnt something about the country through which we were journeying.

The peasants are of a different nationality to any other race in eastern Europe and are called Magyars; but among the nobility there is a large admixture of German blood, the reason for which I learnt later at Buda. The royal family are surnamed Arpad, and it was they who first led the Magyars from their camping grounds in Asia to settle in what was known as the 'Empty Land.' The Magyars were, and still are, horsemen of great skill, and even now, have many of the characteristics of a nomad race.

Under the greatest of their kings, St Stephen, the whole land became Christian. The king then reigning, Bela IV, was his direct descendant. About seventeen years previously there had been great trouble in the country on account of the Tartar invasion—I was to learn much more about this at Buda—but as soon as the barbarians had gone back to Asia, the king had set to work to repairing all the damage done and, as I could see for myself, the country looked prosperous enough.

Night was drawing in as we came to a large village, and my companion suggested our seeking a lodging and spending the night there in preference to a bed under a tree in the open country. We found the church closed, so I knelt for a few moments outside in the porch. As I rose from my knees, I saw an old man of the better-class peasant type talking eagerly to my companion. As I joined them he beamed at me and spoke again, but of course I understood nothing of what he said.

The pedlar turned to me saying: 'This old man insists that we spend the night at his house. He says that it is only a poor place, but he and his wife will give us all the welcome in the world. He is excited at seeing you, Sir, for he says that more than thirty years ago he found two friars in the church porch and that God has blessed him ever since.'

I looked closer at the old man, and his smile of welcome was in itself a pressing invitation. So I nodded to the pedlar. 'Let us take advantage of his invitation and be grateful,' said I, and prepared to follow the old man.

My companion told him what I had said, the peasant gave a joyous chuckle and said something more in a rapid undertone. 'Paul says that his wife, Kinga, will be just as pleased as he is. We are fortunate, Sir.'

Our destination, a wooden house, was not far off. The door opened on to a single room which, in spite of a few hens, looked fairly clean. There was a fire burning on the hearth and something which smelt appetizing was cooking over it. An old woman was stirring a pot which hung on a tripod and, as the door opened, she turned to welcome her husband. Then she caught sight of us and her face was a study; surprise and bewilderment followed by tremendous joy. She hurried to me with outstretched hands.

'Welcome, friend of God,' she cried. 'May he be blessed for sending you. We are only poor folk, but we owe the friars a debt we can never pay; so come in and you shall have the best supper that I can find for you.'

The old man made us sit down on a bench in the hearth place while his wife served stew from the pot on to platters covered with large pieces of bread. We ate our supper there in the hearth place, our platters on our knees; and when we had finished the stew we ate the bread trenchers. After we had finished the old couple had their meal; they would not eat with us.

Afterwards, the old man told us of his first meeting with the friars. He spoke in Magyar, pausing every now and then, for my companion to translate it into lingua franca. So, as far as my memory serves me, I will try to give the story as the peasant told it and as the pedlar translated it to me.

'All this happened a matter of some thirty-five summers ago, when the friars first came to Hungary. We had not long been married, my wife and I, and we were poor enough. I was a herdsman, at work early and late, very often both day and night at calving time.

'I went to Mass at dawn one holy day and hurried home afterwards for something to eat, knowing that I shouldn't get back before nightfall. As I came out of church I noticed two strangers near the bottom; young men in white tunics and long black cloaks. When I passed the church again on my way to the pasture, the young men were still standing in the porch, for the sacristan had cleared away the Mass things and locked the doors. The strangers looked both cold and hungry, and no one seemed to have thought of taking them home and giving them a meal.

'I couldn't leave them standing there so, busy though I was, I went up to them. "Sirs," I said, "will you come home with me? My wife and I are only poor folk but we will do the best we can for you." They thanked me, seeming really grateful for the invitation. They had a hungry look as though they hadn't seen food for long enough. I took them to the cottage, set them before the hearth, just as you are now, and went to find the wife who was washing yarn outside.

"'I've brought home two stranger friars," said I, "can you find them something to eat? They look cold and hungry." "God help us!" she cried, throwing up her hands, "I don't know what I'll do. It's not that I begrudge them anything we have, but that there is nothing in the house to eat but a handful of millet and one or two little fish. And what's that between two hungry men?" says she. "And what's more, we haven't a penny piece in the house to buy any."

"'Cook the scrap of millet and the fish such as they are," I said, "and I'll have one look in the purse, in case there's a penny you've missed." "It's not likely I'd miss a penny," said she with a snort. But, nevertheless, I went to the purse and, sure enough, there were two pennies; actually two pennies. The wife wouldn't believe until she'd seen with her own eyes. Then, while she cooked the fish and spelt, I went to market and bought bread, plenty of it, and wine.

'So, between one thing and another, those friars had a right good meal. And so amazed was I at the two pennies, the men and their appetites that I stayed in the house instead of going on to work. When they had finished and said their grace of thanksgiving, they picked up their sticks and wallets and prepared to set off again. But before going, they blessed us both and asked God to prosper us in all our ways and, specially, that we might never be in want of a meal, or money to buy it.

'We wished them God speed and thought no more about it. But from that day to this we have never gone hungry and there has always been two pence in the purse to buy us anything we wanted. So now you will understand how pleased we are to see your Reverence, and how proud to welcome you to our house.'

I had felt rather shy of accepting the generous hospitality of this man, who obviously had not too much to spare, but after I had heard his story, I was no longer ashamed since he had been so abundantly blessed by my brethren; so my companion and I spent the night before the hearth wrapped in our cloaks and, next morning after we had heard Mass and broken our fast, we went on our way. I added my prayers and blessing to those of my brethren at the express request of the peasant and his wife; though, when I thought of what they were and what I was I felt rather shame-faced at doing so.

I have explained that my recollections are rather like a gallery of pictures and not like a continuous story, so you will understand when I tell you that I remember very little of the remainder of my journey to Buda, except for one curious thing that I noticed.

Some time after mid-day we came on a church standing all alone in a clearing. I know it was afternoon because we were travelling east-south-east and our shadows were lengthening before us. Two or three miles farther on we passed a sizeable village, but it had no church.

'What's the reason for that?' I asked, 'First a church without a village and then a village without a church.'

My companion laughed. 'I've told you that the Magyars are still wanderers at heart,' he replied, 'and this proves it. When they get tired of living in one place they pull their houses to pieces, put them on carts and go off elsewhere; that accounts for their peculiar appearance, they are made to come apart and fix together again easily. But the churches are more solidly built and so they are obliged to leave them behind and travel backwards and forwards, to and from the nearest church.'

Two days later we reached Buda, a large and beautiful city where the king has his palace. On one side of it stretches the Danube; a very broad river, covered with craft of all kinds. On the far shore, almost out of sight, stands Pesth, Buda's twin city. We have priories in both cities, but I was bound for Buda. Farther down the river I saw an island almost covered with a large imposing building.

'That,' said my companion pointing, 'is the Isle of Hares and there King Bela has built a monastery for his daughter Margaret and her companion nuns of the Order of Preachers.'

CHAPTER XIII

What I learnt at the Priory at Buda

It was sundown when my companion left me at the priory door. Of course I invited him in. He thanked me, but said that his visit was a matter of business, and that he would stand a better chance of selling his wares at one of the inns of the city. Earlier in the year messengers from Prague had brought news of my coming, and the welcome I received was most heartening, and it was not many days before I was quite at home there.

I found the friars a fine body of men, but there was no single one among them who made such an impression on me as Jasek Odrowatz, or my friend Albert. This may have been due to myself rather than to the friars, because I had been sent to Hungary to study history and not humanity as at Kracow; and so my mind was occupied with things and peoples rather than with individuals. Besides that, the priory at Buda was the Studium Generale for the Province and most of the community were occupied in study or teaching. So I spent a great part of my time in the library, either in reading or in writing down what I had learnt about peoples and races of men in the east from conversations I had had at different times with the friars. Therefore I fear that this portion of my story will make only dull reading, and that I cannot help.

The priory at Pesth, on the far side of the river, had been founded about twenty-eight years previously. That at Buda was considerably older. The community at the latter place was very proud of the fact that in '54 the Chapter General had been held there; the Chapter in which Master Humbert de Romans had been elected Master General. It was on that occasion that King Bela had given to the Order the monastery that he had built for his daughter, Princess Margaret, and her community on the Isle of Hares; at the same time Sister Margaret made her Solemn Vows in Master Humbert's hands.

Two things in the priory which especially interested me were the school for the study of Arabic there was in the house, and the fact that there were four or five friars there who wore red sashes instead of leather belts. I was told that these were the Fratres Peregrini, specially dedicated to preaching about the heathen nations. There had been one or two of them in many of the bigger priories since master Jordan's time, but Master Humbert was trying to form them into a kind of separate province; not that they were to live in priories apart, but that they were to be directly under the jurisdiction of a special Vicar General. Those I met in Buda had either just returned from a foreign mission, or were preparing to set out on one.

I had not been in Buda long before I began to realize that there was a certain strain and anxiety among the fathers of the community. Their thoughts seemed to be turned east to where the Tartar hordes had disappeared some fifteen years before. There had been no trace of the same strain among the friars of the Polish Province, where they had suffered just as much from Ogdai's invasion. Of course the Poles were of a different nationality, but that hardly accounted for this marked difference in their outlook.

I happened to be glancing through the enactments of Chapters General one day and among those of the previous year I found this: 'We enjoin that the Brethren from Hungary, if they are driven out of their own land, are to be received charitably in the Provinces to which they are sent by the Master General.'

Why Hungary rather than Poland, I asked myself? There must be some added danger to the Province in which I was then living. Was it from the Magyars themselves, or from foreign elements in the country? Was it from the Cumans or the Tartars? Or was there at the time internal feuds and difficulties? Here was a question which had a direct bearing on what I had been told to study, and to which it was necessary for me to find an answer.

So I set to work to find out and note down first all that I could about the Magyars. Next I took the Cumans, then the Tartars, and, lastly, I gathered all I could of what was going on in Hungary at the moment. By comparing facts I was able to draw some probable conclusions. Here, in order, are the facts I found.

THE ORIGIN OF THE MAGYARS. The Magyars of Hungary came originally from the region of the Ural and Altai Mountains; as I already knew, they were nomads and most warlike. Historians say that less is known of their beginnings and settlement in Europe than of any other nation. In early times they were very much under the influence of the Turks. As far as we know, they migrated from Asia in the beginning of the ninth century, and travelled in a north-westerly direction to the Black Sea. Their first settlements were probably made between the rivers Don and Dnieper, and they fought the Greeks to gain possession of this territory. Towards the end of this century, they had reached and laid waste part of the territory of Lewis the German. After that, they captured the land along the banks of the Danube. But before the beginning of the next century, they were, in their turn, conquered by the Bulgarians; and so, under Apad, their great leader, they entered Hungary, and drove out the Bulgarians who were already settled there.

Crossing the Carpathian mountains, they then pushed as far as the River Theiss and into the land of Pannonia, from which place they made raids into the north of Italy; by the beginning of the tenth century they were in possession of Pannonia as far as the River Raab.

About seventy or eighty years later St Adelbert, Bishop of Prague, made a missionary journey into Hungary, converted and baptized the king Geza, with his ten year old son, Stephen. This lad is now known as St Stephen, a canonized king and patron saint of Hungary.

Before the turn of the century, Benedictines from Bohemia had made foundations in Hungary. King Geza married Stephen to Gesela, a Christian princess of the German dynasty.

So much for the early history of the Magyars; on his accession King Stephen proclaimed Christianity to be the national religion, he freed his slaves and caused the Christian religion to be preached everywhere.

THE CUMANS. Here I found a curious mixture of fact and legend. The Cumans were a branch of the Tartars who had settled on both banks of the Volga in the ninth century. Their grazing country was therefore on the eastern and north-eastern confines of Hungary. They were a fierce, warlike and intractable nature, much more so than the Magyars who suffered from their proximity. It had been our Father Dominic's ambition to preach to this people, obviously because it would, in all probability, entail a martyr's death for him. Since the foundation of his Order made this personally impossible, he sent Father Paul in his stead. Paul was a Hungarian who had come to study Canon Law in Bologna, where he had gained his Doctorate. He entered the Order and, on account of his nationality, was chosen to found a Province in Hungary. With him went two other Preachers: Berenger and Sadoc, the last of whom I had met both at Sandomierz and Kracow.

After having gathered several more novices while on their journey, Paul and the friars reached Hungary and founded the first priory at Vezsprem, which was followed by a monastery for our nuns. Paul preached through the country and founded many other houses in the kingdom; then he turned his thoughts to Cumania. For a time, however, he continued to preach in Bosnia, Moravia and

Walacia. It was not until three years had passed that, with several companions, he set out for Cumania.

In this connection I heard a story which the narrator told me was a favorite with Master Humbert. A certain friar was told to go and preach to the Cumans. He found this command so hard that he went to a friend of his, a hermit, and asked him to pray for him, because he had been told to go and preach to the Cumans, and the tribe were so savage and stubborn that it seemed a waste of time to try to convert them.

The hermit promised to pray and, accordingly, spent the following night interceding for his friend. At last, in a vision, God showed him a great river spanned by a bridge. Numbers of religious of different Orders were crossing this bridge, each one alone. The Friars Preachers, however, were crossing not on foot by the bridge, but swimming the river; and certain of them were dragging after them whole boatloads of people. When anyone of these last was overwhelmed by the weight of the boat, he saw Our Lady come to his help, holding the boat and its load in her gentle hands, so that, under her powerful protection, they all reached the farther bank in safety. Afterwards, she led the friars together with those they had brought in their boats to wonderfully pleasant places.

Next day the hermit told the friar of his vision or dream; and the poor man was encouraged to carry out the obedience given him with joyous alacrity, for he now understood that Friars Preachers are called by God to carry heavier loads than other men, but that their labors will be more fruitful and happier in proportion to their labor, since Our Lady herself will help them.

Paul and his companions managed to penetrate the Cuman country on the borders of the Theiss and the Dnieper, but were driven out. A second attempt was made under his direction, though he was unable to go himself, since at the time he was Provincial of Hungary. While on this expedition two of the friars were massacred.

These two Preachers, whose names are not recorded, were the first martyrs of our Order. They were seized and thrown into prison for, in this way, the Cumans hoped to terrify the remaining friars into leaving the country. But when they found that the rest of the company were still preaching quite undeterred, the Cumans first tortured their prisoners and then put them to death.

After the failure of this second expedition, Master Paul handed the government of the Province to Friar Thierry de Poldio and then led a fresh band of missionaries into Cumania. This time, undoubtedly owing to the prayers of the two martyrs, they met with complete success and great numbers of Cumans were converted. One of their leaders named Brutus, or Bruchus, was baptized with a number of his followers. After living as a good Christian for several years, he became ill, received the Last Sacraments, died, and was buried by the friars in a chapel that he had built in honor of Our Lady.

A Cuman noble of much higher rank was baptized later on with nearly a thousand of his followers. His name was Bemborch or Beroch. An imposing ceremony was made of the mass Baptism, and King Andrew of Hungary was Bemborch's godfather.

In what follows, I am leaving factual history for legend. When the Cumans chief was dying, his friends and relatives stood around his couch, and several Friars Preachers were there also. Turning to the friars, he said: 'Send away all the heathen Cumans, because I can see them surrounded by a terrible host of devils. Only the friars are to stay here and the baptized Cumans.' Then later on he spoke again: 'Look!' he said, 'there are the friars we martyred and sent to heaven. They are waiting ready for me, ready to show me the way to the joys of heaven, which in their life-time they preached to us.' Soon afterwards he died in peace and joy and was buried in the chapel in which Bruchus already lay.

To return to facts. Conversions were proceeding so rapidly that Paul asked the Master General to send more and still more friars. In 1234 Pope Gregory IX gave the Cumans a bishop for themselves only, and asked Bela IV to give them their own cathedral city. The friars working in Cumania found that the converted Cumans made excellent catechists.

So much for one chronicler, one with a love for the Cumans; but I found other matter. Among the ordinances of the General Chapter of 1253, there was a note to the effect that the friars' work among these people was often very difficult, for the habits of the Cumans were ferocious; and there were scandals even among the baptized. This gives another aspect of the story, and one which was confirmed by a conversation that I had later on with the Prior Marcellinus.

THE TARTARS. My search for information about the Tartars led me much farther afield than either the Magyars or Cumans. From the era before Christ, at irregular intervals Europe was over-run by hordes of Barbarians from the east: first the Scythians, then the Alani, next the Huns. These last, under Attila, spread over Pannonia.

In the eleventh and twelfth centuries after Christ it was the turn of the Turks, who became masters of the greater part of Asia, including the Holy Land. Just before the start of the thirteenth century, the Turkish empire began to break up, and this was hastened by the invasion of the Monguls, who sweeping through Persia have appeared before Baghdad in this very year 1258. As I am writing this, couriers have even now brought the news.

The armies of these Monguls, or Tartars, are still ranging all over central Asia, spreading as far as China on the east. It was the great Jenghis Khan who, some fifty years ago, gathered the different tribes into one great empire with himself as supreme chief. In 1236, a great expedition westward was organized by his successor, Ogdai, his son, and this was led by Ogdai's nephew Batu. The different chieftains met in Great Bulgaria and captured the cities of Bulgar, Moscow and Vladimir. Then they advanced west and destroyed Kiev. It must have been at this time that Jasek escaped with the statue of Our Lady. There the army divided, one force pushing its way through Poland, while the other crossed the Carpathians into Hungary. The Hungarians were defeated on the River Theiss in 1241, Pesth was captured and the kingdom laid waste. Later in the same year, however, the death of Ogdai obliged Batu and his forces to return to Asia for the election of the Supreme Khan; and Hungary was saved for the time.

SPECIAL FACTS RELATING TO HUNGARY. So far for the general trend of events; my next task was to find information which had special reference to Hungary.

Sometime about eighteen years ago, King Bela heard that there was a tribe of his own Magyar race living in western Asia and still unconverted, so he asked the provincial to send two friars, in the first place on journey of discovery, to find out for certain that the tribe existed and, in the second place, if and when they found them to preach to them and invite them to join their kinsmen in Europe. The two friars, Julian and Bernard, set out and after struggling through almost insurmountable difficulties which resulted in the death of Bernard, Julian at last arrived at the place where the tribe actually lived. He found that single handed he could do little, so he returned to obtain more missionaries.

In Hungary he found everything in a turmoil and no present hope of more missionaries. The Tartars were advancing, and the Cumans fleeing westward to escape them obtained from the king permission to settle in the interior of the country on condition of their receiving mass Baptism. From that time on there is little in the way of written chronicles. The king and his family appear to have taken refuge for a time with the Duke of Austria. Relations between the two rulers became so strained, that the Arpads returned, to be driven south-west by the Tartars, losing battle after battle until at last they took refuge on an Island off Spalato. I learnt more about this when I heard the tale of Princess Margaret.

While he was preparing a fleet of boats to invade the island, Batu heard of the death of the Khan Ogdai, and the victorious Tartars melted away like snow in summer. It was during this time that Master Paul of Hungary was killed with ninety other friars by the Tartars. The chronicles were full of tales of massacres, but I will only give an account of one to serve as an example.

Married women, girls and a crowd of those unfit to fight and who had taken refuge in the church were burnt to death. To a man the Tartars put to the sword nobles and peasants, knights and whole colleges of priests. They committed unspeakable crimes in the churches, violating holy images and destroying relics and vestments. They raped women and, after they had satisfied their lust, took them into the churches and killed them.

A Hungarian noble, whose name is not known for certainty, but which is conjectured to be Buzad Banzio, had joined the Order. When the other friars left the town, he begged to be allowed to stay behind to help those inhabitants who were unable to leave. When the Tartars broke into the church, they found him lying prostrate in prayer with outstretched arms before the altar. After the enemy had left the town, the poor people whom he had stayed to help crept back to the church, to find his dead body literally hacked to pieces.

When the news of his martyrdom reached his brethren, one of them, a special friend of his, lying prostrate before the altar, begged God with tears to show him how it was that such a man should meet with such a death. For three days and nights he prayed and on the third night he had a vision, in which he saw his friend, who said to him: 'Ought not Christ to have suffered these

105

things and so to have entered into his glory? The sufferings of this life are not worthy to be compared with the glory to come which shall be revealed to us.' So saying, he disappeared, leaving his friend comforted and at peace.

One day as I was searching among the manuscripts, I came on a list of martyrs among the Friars Preachers in the Province of Hungary and its confines during the twenty-three years following their coming into the country in 1221.

There were the two nameless protomartyrs whom I have already mentioned; then Paul of Hungary and his ninety companions killed by the Tartars; there were a hundred and ninety others killed at the same time as Buzad Banzio. There were an uncounted number of others killed by the Cumans.

There was Father Conrad Marpurgensio the Teutonic, the first Inquisitor of the Faith in the east who was killed by heretics. Another Inquisitor, who has been consecrated bishop, because he preached the Faith and refused to be silent, was stoned to death and afterwards brutally mutilated. Another Hungarian Inquisitor, Father Nicholas, was flayed alive. Some time before 1250, a namesake and fellow-countryman of Paul of Hungary was bound alive to a stake and burned to death. Some time between 1240 and the same year, 1250, on the borders of Hungary and Bosnia, the invading Tartars captured and drowned thirty-two Friars Preachers. The manuscript tells of a prodigy which was seen that same year. Over the place where the friars were drowned, thirty-two lights appeared.

I realize, of course, that this list of martyrs is very incomplete and that there are probably hundreds more whose names will never be known to us. When the Tartars destroyed our priories, they burned all the manuscripts they could find with lists of names, professions and the like; so we have only a small proportion that our brethren managed to save. When you add to this that I myself am writing from memory, you will understand what an incomplete list I am giving.

All this history I certainly found most interesting, but my studies were not leading me very far. I could find no explanation which would account for the fact that Hungary was considered to be in greater danger than other eastern countries, Poland for instance. I could only conjecture that it was possibly something which was happening in the actual present, and of course I could learn nothing of this from histories and chronicles. My only hope was to get the answer from a living Hungarian, and one, moreover, who was well informed. But the men at the priory were all so busy that I hardly liked to trouble them with my questions. All that was left for me, therefore, was to await my opportunity. In the meantime, I began to transcribe the story of Friar Anzelinus; a story which will be given just as I transcribed it, rather farther on in this book.

It is one of the few papers that I have kept.

CHAPTER XIV

What I learnt from the Provincial:
Father Marcellus

It happened one day that the provincial, Father Marcellus, being in residence at Buda, was obliged to go out on business; and to my surprise this important man asked me, a nobody, to go out with him. I was as pleased as I was surprised, for the provincial, besides being a great traveler, was not only a very learned man, a good preacher and an excellent confessor, but also very approachable and companionable. If I saw an opportunity, I should not be afraid of putting to him my questions concerning the mysterious danger which appeared to threaten Hungary more than other eastern countries.

As we came out of the door, he stood for a minute looking out over the great river, alive with craft and sparkling in the late autumn sunshine. 'See,' he said, pointing southward. 'Look how the sun is shining on those roofs. That is our nuns' monastery on the Isle of Hares.'

'I have often looked across and thought what a lovely place it looked,' I answered. 'I know the nuns are enclosed, are we ever allowed to go there?'

The provincial nodded. 'Yes, with permission,' he said. 'When I am at home, I am one of their confessors. One of these days I will take you over with me to visit them.'

After I had thanked him, he added reflectively: 'They're wonderful people, and I never go over without feeling an absolute worm. Here am I, a strong man and quite fit for any austerities, but these delicate little women beat me all along the line, though most of them belong to the Hungarian nobility and are brought up to every luxury. You should see the hard lives they live and seem to enjoy. Little Margaret, a princess, is the most humble and penitential of them all. Yet there is no show about them, just gaiety.'

This promise of a visit pleased me greatly, for we had no Preacheresses in England and I was interested in them and the life they live; more especially as I knew that Prouille was earliest in time and was our Father Dominic's first foundation.

But I knew I could discuss the nuns at any time and with anybody; the fathers were only too ready to talk about the wonderful women on Hares' Isle. The important question I had on my mind, one that had a direct bearing on the subject I had been told to study, was something that, in my opinion, the provincial was best qualified to answer.

'As you know, Father,' I said, 'I have been sent here to study all that I can about the peoples of Eastern

Europe and their beginnings. I have found out something about the Magyars, the Cumans and the Tartars. The other day I happened to come on last year's Chapter enactments. Among them I found a clause dealing with this Province. If the Fathers are driven out of Hungary, they are to be received with charity in any other Province to which they may be sent. Why is the danger greater here than in—Poland, for instance?'

The provincial looked at me rather amused I thought, in the same disconcerting way that the Polish provincial looked. What was it in my questions, or in myself, that they found funny? However, he answered me quite seriously.

'There is a passage in the bible, Thomas, about a city divided against itself being unable to stand. That is what is happening here.'

'Surely no more so than in Poland,' I protested, 'for in that country territory seems to be forever changing hands. Today such and such provinces belong to Little Poland, for instance; tomorrow they belong to Great Poland, or Silesia or anywhere else you like to mention. And as for pride and independence and touchiness!'

The provincial laughed. 'Nevertheless, the Poles are all of one race—Slavs—and they have only one quarrel with our friars, and that is that a proportion of them are Germans. They will disagree violently among themselves, but if danger threatens them from outside, they will stand by one another through thick and thin. It is like the tale of the husband and wife who fought day and night with each other, but both turned at once on the man who, hearing the wife's screams, rushed in to protect her. But here—God help us!'

'But you are all Magyars, are you not? A race which is much more distinctive than the Slavs, who belong to half a dozen countries.'

'We are Magyars—and the rest, Thomas. *Now* the majority of our men of better standing are Germans; a race that does not mix well with the Magyar. There were a certain number before '42, but since the Tartar invasion they have greatly increased. The king was determined that the country should make a quick recovery, so he invited Germans who are good, hardworking farmers to settle in large tracts of devastated land. The Germans are of one stock, the Magyars of another, so no love or loyalty is lost between them.

'To add to the confusion, when the Tartars advanced westward, the Cumans fled from our eastern boundaries where they had settled. King Bela allowed them to remain in Hungary proper, on condition that they agreed to mass Baptism of the tribe. Fine Christians they made under those conditions! After the Tartars left, they remained in large tracts of central Hungary. Some are practicing Christians, some are mere nominal ones, and some are frankly pagans. They feel, with some show of reason, that they were not fairly treated during the invasion; they were used as cover for our retiring forces. So, you can see, that they are not to be trusted if the Tartars come back!'

'I understand now,' said I, 'why the friars here are in greater danger than in other countries.'

The provincial smiled: 'Sister Margaret hopes that if the Tartars come she will be tortured and mutilated, she has even told us her desires in detail. However, she is kind enough to say that, for the sake of the country, she hopes they won't come.'

I exclaimed in horror: 'What a dreadful wish!' I said.

The provincial's smile broadened to a grin. 'Wait until you see her,' he remarked. Then he added in a different tone: 'Talking of Margaret brings me to a much more serious reason for discord in the country than those I have told you of; one leading to increasing danger. And that reason is the royal Arpads themselves. Stephen, their son, is a great problem, a cause of anxiety to both father and mother. He and the King don't agree at all. Bela is a very good Christian and a great friend of our Order, while Stephen is hand-in-glove with the Cumans; he has had more than one Cuman mistress, and there is question now of his marrying one of their princesses. Before marrying him she will be baptized, of course; but from what I know of the tribe, there it will end. Added to this, Prince Stephen who, as you know, is the eldest son and heir to the throne, has an active, personal dislike of his father and, by all accounts, is none too fervent a Christian himself. So here we are: Magyars hating the German settlers; Cumans hating both Germans and Magyars; and the King and his heir at cross-purposes. If the Tartars return what hope is there of our driving them out? Our only hope would lie in our complete unity; and that will never be without a radical change everywhere.'

'No wonder that the Chapter made a special enactment to give some protection to the Hungarian Province,' I said half to myself; then I asked aloud: 'If the Tartars invade in strength, will the Province as a body leave the country?'

'The greater number will certainly go,' answered the
provincial. 'We lost so heavily in the '42 invasion that we
can afford to leave behind only those men who are
necessary to serve the convents and the people. The
others, students and professors, must go so as to preserve
a nucleus from which to rebuild the Province.'

'Then you will leave the nuns behind?' I asked,
surprised and a little shocked, for I hardly thought that in
England we should do such a thing.

'There is no other course open to us. We have three
monasteries of women here: at Zara, Veszprim—and on
the Isle of Hares. Suppose we were to take the nuns with
us, what then? It will be a dangerous exodus even for
men, wandering across Hungary, among such as the
Cumans. Think of such a flight for women. What if they
fell sick, or strayed and got lost? Besides, there will be a
great chance of the Tartars catching up with us, and then?
No. Undoubtedly our nuns take a risk in remaining, as
well as the friars who look after them. But the risk of their
remaining is not nearly so great as that they will incur by
taking to flight. There is always a chance of the Tartars
passing by the monasteries. And, suppose the worst
happens, that the convents are captured and there is a
general massacre, even so the nuns will suffer less than if
they were to die—or worse—one by one on the journey.'

I said nothing, but it struck me that either alternative
was pretty grim, I was sorry for the nuns. Into my mind
came unbidden the remembrance of Friar Kazemierz at
Sandomierz and his chivalry and his worship of the Lady
Truth. For all they thought so much of them, the
practical notions of these friars with regard to the nuns

did not accord very well with what I had heard that day from the young man. Where was one to find a synthesis?

The provincial did his business and then we returned to the priory, and as we walked we talked of this and that. If I remember right Father Marcellus asked me questions about England and our houses there, chiefly Oxford and London. But there was nothing of sufficient importance for me to retain it in my memory.

When I reached home, I went to the church and remained there, thinking of what I had heard that morning, and I found it all most disquieting. I could understand a fight; as a youngster I had enjoyed many a rough and tumble, and I had been mixed up in a brawl with quarter staves and broken heads above once. Of course, as a religious, that was now barred to me, nevertheless, if I had not been one I could have taken my share with zest even now. Martyrdom I had accepted as part of my day's work when I took the habit. But this business of fleeing before an enemy seemed to me dishonorable, and certainly distasteful to my pride. In travelling through a wild country, the friars were doing a most difficult thing and one which could not add to their credit. Moreover, death on the journey gave no promise of immediate entrance into heaven as martyrdom did. The whole thing was beyond me, and with a half despairing glance at the tabernacle I left the church.

As it was the fasting season and the midday meal was not before two or three o'clock, I went to the library, took out Father Simon's manuscript about Frater Anzelinus's mission to the Tartars and began to study it, before transcribing. The manuscript did not in any way add to my comfort.

These things were only the beginnings of my trouble. Far worse was to follow.

Chapter XV

The History of the Mission of Father Anzelinus
Which I found in the Library at Buda

This happened during my stay at Buda, but is, I fancy, out of its chronological order.

I was looking through the manuscripts in the library one day when I came across a notice of a Papal mission sent to the Tartars some thirteen years previously. Standing on the shelf near it was a second manuscript which gave the whole story in detail. I found it so fascinating that I transcribed it and, strangely enough, kept it through my journeys until my return to England, adding queries of my own.

This is what I copied from the first manuscript: 'In 1245, at the Council of Lyons, Pope Innocent IV sent legates to the Tartars, who had been devastating great tracts in Europe, requesting them for the future to refrain from such carnage.

'Four legates were chosen from the Order of Preachers: Anzelinus, Alexander Albert, Simon, and Guicard of Cremona. There were also two Franciscans;

as well as several more friars from the same and other Orders.'

This was another notice: 'When the Tartars returned to Asia, all the European nations were filled with apprehension and the Christian princes were terrified lest they should return. So they consulted together and approached Innocent IV who was holding a Council at Lyons. He sent Father Anzelinus, a Friar Preacher, together with several more to meet the Tartars.

'They went through Germany and Bohemia to Breslau and were received with Honor by Boleslas, Duke of Silesia. From there they went to the court of Conrad, Duke of Masovia, where they also received a cordial welcome.' (Obviously, these were the Christian princes who had taken counsel together.) 'Their next stopping place was Kracow, where they received a kind welcome from Boleslas the Chaste, his mother Grimislava, and the Lord Bishop Prandota, the Ordinary. The embassy was provided with a number of beautiful furs, over and above what they already carried or were able to buy, because the Tartars would consider it an insult if they came empty-handed.

'From Kracow they went to Sandomierz; and Vasiko, a Russian Prince, a nephew of Boleslas, invited them to Kiev. There they obtained horses for the journey, as wet and snow made travel on foot impossible.'

This is a concise account of the setting of the embassy. The remainder of the story I copied from the second manuscript, which gives in detail the work of the friars and the fate of the embassy.

'At length they left Kiev and came at last to Persia, where they founded an encampment with several Tartar generals, under a prince, Bayothnoy by name. They asked these people to take them to the Khan or supreme ruler of the Tartars.

'When the message was brought to him, Bayothnoy went to his tent to dress himself in cloth-of-gold, whilst his lieutenants also put on rich apparel. Then he sent one of his nobles to the friars together with his chief counselor and interpreters. After the customary salutations, the Tartar enquired whose messengers the friars were. Frater Anzelinus, their leader, answered for them all: I am the messenger of my Lord the Pope, who is held among Christians to have the highest dignity of any man on earth and is looked upon by them as their Father and Lord to whom they all show reverence.

'On hearing this the Tartars became very angry and said: How can you speak so arrogantly, saying that your Pope is greater than any other man? Does he not know that the Khan is the son of god, and that Bayothnoy and Batu' (he was the leader when the Tartars invaded Hungary) 'are his princes, and thus their names are known and their fame spread everywhere? Anzelinus answered: Who is the Khan? And who are Bayothnoy and Batu? Our Lord the Pope does not so much as know their names. But this he has heard from many, and this he does know, that there are certain barbarous people called the Tartars who, some time ago, came from the far east, and who conquered countries which belong to his Lord and, sparing no one, have killed an infinite multitude of men. If we had known the name of the Khan and those of his princes, their names would have been written on the wrapping of the letters we have brought. But their distress at the slaughter of men, specially Christians, has moved the Cardinals to consult together, and to send us to the first Tartar army we could find, to beg the general and all under his command, to cease from slaughter for the future, and to repent for what they have done in the past; as you will see by the tenor of these letters. We beg you, therefore, to receive these letters from our Lord the Pope and, after having read them, to reply by messenger, or even to send a verbal reply by us.

'When this speech had been interpreted to the princes they returned to their chief. After some time had elapsed, having changed their garments for new ones, they returned to the friars and said: We wish to know one thing: whether this man, your Lord the Pope, has sent any gifts we can carry to our Lord Bayothnoy? Frater Anzelinus answered: We have brought nothing from our Lord the Pope, as he is not accustomed to send gifts to infidels, especially when he does not even know their names.' (I wondered what had happened to the furs which were mentioned in the other manuscript. But this is not the only discrepancy; it is difficult to report accurately what one learns by word of mouth.) 'It should rather be the other way about, and you should send gifts to him. Then they all returned again to Bayothnoy's tents and, after some delay, again appeared before the embassy in new raiment.

'They said: How can we for shame take your Lord's letter empty-handed to our master? Such a thing has never happened before. Frater Anzelinus replied:

Everywhere it is an approved custom among Christians that an accredited messenger should deliver letters with his own hand to the one to whom they are addressed; if we are not permitted to go to your master the Khan unless we have presents for him, will it be pleasing to you all if we give them to Bayothnoy, for him to pass on? But, in addition to the letters, there will be many questions to ask; whether, as heretofore, it will be unsafe for the Franks to cross to Syria? And what pledge will he give of his good faith?

'After they heard him, the leaders went back again and, having put on still more new robes, they told the friars: If you wish to see our Lord and give your letters, you must adore him as the son of god, ruling over the whole earth. First, you must genuflect three times, for so the Khan has commanded. This perplexed the legates, who began to discuss among themselves whether such homage would involve idolatry. Frater Guicard, who knew the customs of the Tartars because he had been teaching in Georgia where the Preachers have a house, answered that a genuflection did not imply idolatry, but it did imply the entire subjection of the Pope to the Khan. On hearing this, the rest decided unanimously that they would rather be beheaded than give a sign which would be a scandal to Georgians, Armenians, Greeks, Persians, Turks and all eastern nations. So Anzelinus, having the consensus of the others, replied:

'We cannot do as you ask, because by this we shall belittle our own Lord; however, we are willing to offer your princes the reverence which we show to our own kings and princes. But we would rather die than do this other thing that you command. If, on the contrary, your

121

Lord Bayothnoy desires to be a Christian, then we will not only genuflect to him and to each one of you but, for God's sake, we will kiss the feet of even the least among you.

'This made the Tartars furious and they shouted: Do you think we would become dogs of Christians as you are? Is not your Pope a dog and are not all the rest of you dogs? Anzelinus gave no further answer, except to repeat his refusal to adore Bayothnoy. In fact, they were making such a furious din that he could not make himself heard. So the chiefs went back to Bayothnoy again.

'When Bayothnoy heard what his lieutenants had to say, he was mad with rage. Three times he ordered the death of the messengers, having no objection to the shedding of innocent blood; but his officers did not agree with him as they feared to infringe the rights of messengers.' (The embassy must have had some friend among the Tartars, possibly a renegade Christian; how could they otherwise have known what happened at a distance? Frater Simon was the author of the manuscript and an eyewitness. The remainder is so circumstantial that he would hardly have invented this scene.) 'Certain of them spoke in this fashion: Do not let us kill all of them, but only two, sending the others back to the Pope. Others said: Let us flay their leader, stuff his skin with straw and make the others carry this back to the Pope. Others said: Let us have two killed by the soldiers and send the others back to the Franks.

'Others again said: Let us take the two highest in rank and show them to the army. Let them be placed in front of our engines of war, so that they may be accounted killed, not by us, but by the machine. However, in the end, Bayothnoy's decision prevailed that all should be killed for refusing to adore him. At length, when all was settled, the senior of Bayothnoy's six wives, she who had charge of the feeding of the messengers spoke thus: If these messengers are killed, the fact will soon be public everywhere, and everyone will be horrified and disgusted. You will lose all the gifts you are accustomed to receive from foreigners; and any messengers you may send on your side will be killed without mercy. Then the man whose charge it was to be responsible for messengers to the army, spoke thus to Bayothnoy: Do you remember how angry the Khan was with me when some messengers were killed by your orders, and how severely I was punished? If, therefore, you order the death of these messengers, I will have no part in their execution, but will take to flight to preserve my innocence. I shall go to the Khan and accuse you in full council of this unspeakable crime. These arguments had the effect of calming Bayothnoy.

At last, after a long delay, the leaders returned to the friars with their interpreters and, after describing their Lord's anger, said that if the friars could in no wise genuflect before him and adore him, in what manner did they show honor to their lords at home. Furthermore, they said: If we allow you to come into the presence of our Lord, what honor and reverence will you show him? Friar Anzelinus threw back his capuce and bowing his head, answered: This is the way in which we salute our superiors; and, unless you force us to do otherwise, this is the way in which we will greet your Lord Bayothnoy.

'Next they enquired in what way Christians adore God. Anzelinus replied that some prostrate and some kneel, some show reverence and adoration in one way, some in another. He added: Many adore *your* master through fear, as servants and slaves. But our Lord Pope does not rule through fear, nor exact adoration by tyranny. Nor does he ask what the Khan demands in these matters. Then others asked Anzelinus: Christians adore wood and stone made in the likeness of a cross, and that Bayothnoy would disdain to do, because the Khan is the son of god, to be adored as such. Anzelinus answered: We do not adore wood and stones, but the sign of the cross which is carved on them; the cross on which Our Lord, Jesus Christ, was hung, whose hands and feet adorned it like precious pearls; his Blood shed for our salvation consecrated it; and for these reasons we cannot adore your Khan.

'The embassy returned to report to Bayothnoy. After a while they came back and told the friars that Bayothnoy had ordered them to prepare to go to the Khan, lord and ruler of all Tartary; then they would see his greatness and their eyes would be opened. So they would be able themselves to present their letters to the Khan.

'But Anzelinus saw through the malice of Bayothnoy, and how he would warn the Khan of their coming so that he would be prejudiced against them; therefore he replied: As my Lord the Pope does not even know the name of your Khan, he sent us to the first Tartar general that we should meet, therefore, I neither can nor will go to your Khan. I will give my letters and message to your master, Bayothnoy, since this is what I have been told to do.

'They took this message back to Bayothnoy, and at length, returning, told the legates that the letters must be delivered to them, in their character as messengers of the general, to examine. So Anzelinus, being denied access to Bayothnoy, gave them the letters, although it was contrary to the approved custom. It was not long before the messengers came back, saying: The letters of the Lord Pope are not written in Persian, and they must be translated into that language before Lord Bayothnoy can understand them.

'So Anzelinus and the other three friars were brought into the presence of Bayothnoy, but at a great distance from him, and standing there in the full glare of the sun, surrounded by a great crowd, as well as by the interpreters and scribes, they translated the Pope's letter word by word, through the interpreters. All was written down by the notaries, as it was given to them by the Greek and Turkish interpreters. The finished translation was read to Bayothnoy, who told them to give this message to the friars: Bayothnoy commands you to choose two of your number, who will go straight to the Khan with these letters. They two will give him your Lord's letters, will see the power and glory of the Khan and will bring back the answer.

To this, Friar Anzelinus replied: We have told you that we have no orders to go to the Khan, so we will not go unless you take us by force. Nor will we separate one from the other as we are a single embassy.

'The messengers took this answer to their master, and the notary who remained behind with the friars, though his words were deceitful and flattering, criticized Anzelinus for what he had done and said, trying by every means to persuade him to adore Bayothnoy. Friar Anzelinus told him: I believe that what I have said has been heard by a number of people, and that the truth ought to be known by the Tartars. But I see that it has been falsified to them, and that truth is neither loved nor respected by you. I have stated two facts: first, that our Lord the Pope is in Christian eyes the greatest of men, and second, that he knows neither the Khan nor Bayothnoy, and these facts are most important for them to understand. In defense of the liberty of truth and faith I stand here fearing no mortal man.

'As it was now evening, the friars were allowed to go, being told that on the following day the notary would come and read to them the letter that Bayothnoy was sending to the Khan to be used publicly. Furthermore, they were warned to remember all that was therein written.

'The next day passed exactly like the previous one. In the late evening the scribe read them the translation of the letter written to the Khan, and the friars were sent fasting to their tents, a long distance from that of Bayothnoy. Four days later the friars Anzelinus and Guicard were brought to Bayothnoy's tent and, through the chief interpreter, were asked the same questions about the Pope's letter, to which they gave the same answer. The friars were then told that they would be summoned later, as they said they had come to see the Tartar army. As our whole army is not gathered here, they were told, you cannot see them now, and until such a time as they are you must not leave. Anzelinus said: From the very first, we told you we did not come for the purpose of seeing the army, but in order to deliver our Lord the Pope's letter and carry back your answer. The messengers went back to the general and the friars were left standing in the hot sun until mid-afternoon, when they were sent back to their tents, having achieved nothing. This went on for days on end, the waiting friars being mocked and treated as dogs by the Tartars.

'And so, almost daily, they went to the place where they were to meet the leaders and stood from dawn to midday, and sometimes on into the afternoon, in the heat of the sun, through the months of June and July. Each day they asked for an answer to their letter, but waited for it in vain, until in the end they returned almost starving to their tents, sometimes without anyone speaking a word to them. Bayothnoy took this way of showing his malice. Patiently and humbly the friars endured his spite and bad temper and showed, in this way, their skill in making a virtue of necessity.

'At length, after five weeks waiting, they learnt that Bayothnoy's letter was ready for the Pope and they thought that they would be allowed to leave on the feast of St John the Baptist. But three days later the permission was withdrawn, and they were told that no one might leave the encampment, since it was understood that a certain high-ranking officer of the Khan, the son of god, a man named Augutha, was coming to visit the army. Some even affirmed that his master had made him ruler of Georgia.

'This Augutha was one of the Khan's chief councilors, who knew the answer that his master wished to be sent to the Lord Pope and, as Bayothnoy asserted, he brought new orders from the Khan to be promulgated everywhere. Bayothnoy wished the friars to understand that these same orders were to be handed to the Pope's messengers, to be by them transmitted to him. Daily Bayothnoy and his chieftains prepared for Augutha, setting a feast with quantities of asses' milk and a great array of food. Therefore, though they had license to do so, he refuse the friars permission to depart until this man should come with, it may be, fresh orders from the Khan, perhaps, even, as some thought most likely, commanding the death of the legates.

'For three weeks more, the friars submitted to the tyrant, waiting from day to day, humbly and patiently, standing upright and motionless in the sun, living on dry bread and a short measure of water, sometimes scarcely sufficient to sustain life, and for lack of bread often fasting until evening. Sometimes they drank goats' milk and ate the flesh of suckling calves, and occasionally they had flesh meat of coarse quality to eat. Mostly, they drank water only, though occasionally, to show them some small measure of compassion, it was mixed with sour milk. There was no question of their having wine.

'Friar Anzelinus, having in mind the coming of winter, and that, by reason of this delay, they would lose the opportunity of the easier return by sea, and be forced to go overland, begged an influential man to intercede with Bayothnoy for the friars, and to beg that they might be allowed to depart. Being anxious to make up for lost time and get away quickly, although he was short of everything he promised the official a gift if he would help them. So the man went to Bayothnoy and spoke fair words to him, suggesting that the letters the general had already written should be sent, and the friars be permitted to leave with them instead of waiting for others.

'Now, although the letters were finished and the messengers named and all arranged for the journey, it happened on the very day arranged for their departure that Augutha arrived, accompanied by a relative of the Sultan of Aleppo and a brother of the Sultan of Mostoal, formerly called Nivinive. These two men were sent from the Khan to pay homage and, besides tribute, they brought gifts. So they came into the presence of Bayothnoy and offered him many presents, making the three genuflections and, with their heads bowed to the ground, adoring to the order of the Khan.

'Bayothnoy and his chieftains were overjoyed at the coming of Augutha and his companions, and they made a feast according to their custom, with asses' milk for drink, and accompanied by the singing of songs which sounded more like dirges. Neighboring Tartars, with their wives, came to swell the crowd and all negotiations with the friars were postponed. The feast continued for seven days with eating, drinking and wailing songs until, on the octave day, which was the feast of St James, the friars were given free and complete license to depart with the messengers who took the letter of Bayothnoy and that of the Khan, called the letter of god, to the Pope.

'Friar Anzelinus was absent three years and seven months before he returned to the Pope, Friar Alexander Albert a slightly shorter time, and Simon two years and six weeks.

'This is a copy of the letter sent by Bayothnoy to the Pope:

'By divine disposition of the Khan, sent by Bayothnoy: Know, O Pope, these words. Your messengers came and presented your letters to us. Your messengers addressed us in high sounding phrases; we do not know if this was by your order, or whether they spoke thus of their own accord. In your letter you wrote thus: You have killed and destroyed many men. God's precept and his commandment, that of him to whom belongs the whole world (obviously the Khan) is this. Whosoever will listen to the commandment of him who is lord of the whole world is virtuous. Whosoever does not listen to his commandment shall be destroyed. Now, with regard to this command and precept, we reply: If you wish to rule over land and sea, it is necessary that you, O Pope, should come to us personally and so approach him who is the real ruler of the earth. If you adhere to your God's precept and do not listen to that of him who rules the whole world, we shall not know this, but our god knows. Therefore, before you come, you must send legates to signify to us whether you are coming or not, and if you wish to be in union of friendship with us, or at enmity. Send the required answer without delay. This order we are sending by Aybeg and Sargis, in July, on the twentieth day of the moon. Written in the encampment in the territory of Sitis.

'Here is a copy of the letter of the Khan to Bayothnoy, which was to be sent on to the Pope. The tartars call it the letter of god.

'Through the precept of god, Jenghis Khan, the gentle and venerated son of god, says that god is above all things; the immortal god and Jenghis Khan the sole lord of the world. We desire all to hear these things, both in the provinces that obey us and those which rebel against us. Therefore, O Bayothnoy, you must notify them that this is the command of the divine and immortal god. Straightway make known to them your message (i.e., that the Khan shall cease from killing Christians) and my orders, wherever it is possible for you to send messengers. Whosoever refuses to obey me shall be slain and his lands laid waste. And I certify to you that whoever does not hear my commandment shall be deaf, and whoever sees it and does not obey shall be blind, and whoever obeys, but knowing of my command for peace does not make it, shall be lame. This is my commandment, to be brought to the knowledge of all, both learned and ignorant. Whoever hears and fails to observe it shall be destroyed and die. Make this known, O Bayothnoy, and let whoever desires his house to flourish carry out my command. He who wishes to serve us may be sure of safety and honor. And whoso refuses to obey, following his own will, you must destroy.'

When I had finished my transcript, I read it over and over again, and each time I re-read it I felt more uneasy about the whole matter. Friar Anzelinus and his companions had accomplished nothing. They had said little else except their reiterated assertions that their duty was to follow the commands of the Pope to the letter. They had not preached and they had made no conversions. In fact the only apparent result of their journey was to have turned the minds of the Tartars still more utterly against Christianity. They had been treated with contempt and ignominy of every kind and finally, their mission a complete failure, they had returned to Europe with a letter for the Pope which was one long insult.

To come still more to the concrete: they had done what they had been told to do and their fate might have been that of any Friar Preacher. Suppose that one day I should be called upon to go upon such a useless mission; very unlikely, but, considering my Profession and what I had learnt was expected of our friars in this part of Europe, by no means impossible. Hard blows I could understand; martyrdom was part of the day's work; but this costly ignominious failure to carry out something which had no connection with preaching or teaching, seemed to me something which no Dominican should be expected to undergo. And yet, because of their vow of obedience, on the other hand, these brethren of mine could in conscience have done no other.

I found eastern Europe a thorny spot, full of insoluble problems. I heartily wished myself back in England; a place that I understood.

NOTE. Jenghis Khan died in 1237, his son, the drunken Ogdai, about 1243. Either the name was used as a generic term for the chief Khan—Malvenda gives it GHINGISCAM—of this is a transcriber's error. Malvenda, from whom I took the account, says he copied it from the 'libellus' of Friar Simon, who was one of the legates accompanying Friar Anzelinus.

Chapter XVI

How I Went to the Isle of Hares

All the autumn, and indeed through the winter as well, whenever the weather allowed of him doing so, the provincial was busy in making a visitation of his province, and arranging with the priors of the different houses to send out parties on preaching expeditions in the spring. He had to decide which route each should take and how long each was to be absent, so that there might be no overlapping. When he happened to be in Buda, he had to superintend the making of records and interview the novices and students. Therefore he was obliged to leave the Preacheresses to the care of the prior and two or three of the senior fathers and there was no question raised of my going to St Mary's; indeed I thought that the promise for me to do so was quite forgotten.

I settled in for the winter and set to work to study and to transcribe what I thought might be of use to me. I also joined the school of Arabic; not that I expected to be sent farther east, but one never knew. Who would have guessed three years ago that I should ever have found myself in Poland and Hungary? I also learnt to speak a little Magyar and improved my German; but when we spoke among ourselves, just as in Kracow, the language in common use was Latin.

I must confess that I was lonely, for among those who lived constantly in the priory there were few except Masters, too much my senior and too learned to be companions, and students who had not yet come to grips with reality. I often longed for my friend Albert. My greatest trouble was that during the whole of this time, there remained in the back of my mind a picture of Father Anzelinus and his companions, standing for days on end in that wild, treeless country, sunbaked and half starved, listening to the jeers of the barbarian soldiers— and all this patient heroism to end in failure!

We must all reach the mental stature of adults and sacrifice the milk of babes for the meat of the strong; but for many of us the business of growing up is not an easy one. And because I was inclined to be dogmatic and much too sure of myself and my own infallibility, I felt the chisel on the hard stone of my nature bitterly.

For some unknown reason I also felt the winter weather. Of course it was much colder than in England, but so had been the previous winter in Prague. There I had enjoyed the dry healthy climate, so different to our raw penetrating cold, but here in Buda I was chilled to the bone most of the time and, somehow, I lacked courage to warm myself by taking brisk walks in the good air. This inertia of body was the result, I fancy, of lowness of mind. I was in some sort of trouble, which I know now to be growing pains, that I found it impossible to explain, for I thought that not one of those good men around me would understand it. They were facing real difficulties and were prepared to fly or to remain behind to be killed in Hungary; to be martyrs or fugitives just as obedience required. I thought that my theoretical troubles would sound to them ridiculous; for there was no real question of my being either a martyr or a fugitive.

I am ashamed to say that by the time spring came I was interested neither in budding trees nor in any other outside thing. So when, one bright day in early May, the provincial sent for me, what he might want was, in my eyes, a matter of no importance whatever.

When I reached his room, I was conscious of being the object of scrutiny, but when he began to speak, smiling, it was about something that I had almost forgotten.

'I have not forgotten the promise I made to you that you should visit our nuns, but since last summer I have not been able to go myself, though I know they have been expecting me. However, I have to go into the country on business today. A man who lives close to the priory, a good friend of ours, has offered me his horse and cart. I shall come back past the bridge to the island and shall call at St Mary's for an hour or so to see them and give them a conference. Two of the young friars will bring you to the bridge early tomorrow afternoon. You can come over with me and I'll drive you home before dark.'

I thanked the provincial and left his room a different man. It was humiliating to find that a little kind attention and the fulfillment of a promise when I had lost hope of it should have made such a difference to me; but there it was. At the bottom of my heart I was really anxious to see the Isle of Hares and meet our nuns. When one or two of our men remarked on my changed face I felt still more ashamed; but there it was again, and I could only make the best of it.

We set off immediately after dinner on the next day, walking briskly through the city, keeping close to the river bank. The thaw had set in a month previously and the river was crowded with craft of all kinds and there was loading and unloading on every quay. My two companions, Brothers Stephen and Bernard, were senior students, entertaining and —like all young men, myself included—very ready to discuss everything and very dogmatic in the conclusions they drew. I learnt quite a deal about affairs that afternoon which I certainly should not have learnt in any other way.

'Have you ever seen Preacheresses before?' asked Stephen and, on my saying that I had not, he added, 'Then you will be interested. In some ways they are like us and in others quite different. The only certain thing is that they are much better than we are.'

I made no answer, but I thought to myself that they would have to be very good indeed to improve on the Hungarian friars; for I could admire, even though I could not understand.

'The nuns of St Mary's have always been under the jurisdiction of the provincial,' remarked Bernard. 'The king made that a condition when he handed over the monastery at the General Chapter, and he could not have chosen a better moment, though I suppose he did not know this. For my part I don't like the idea of our having charge of nuns. We are preachers, not nuns' confessors.'

'Aren't all the nuns' monasteries under the jurisdiction of the Order?' I asked, for I remembered Prouille and St Sixtus.

'Yes, they were in the early days,' answered Bernard, 'but the beginnings were small. Later, when preaching, missionary work and teaching in the universities grew much heavier, many of the fathers thought that the care of nuns was too great an addition to their other work and incompatible with it.'

'For my part,' chimed in Stephen, 'I can never understand why the friars objected. After all, as well as preaching to sinners and pagans, it brought us in touch with people who were much better than we are, and in that it was a definite help to us.'

Bernard laughed. 'That, my dear fellow,' he said, 'is because you are more teacher than preacher. A Master's chair and the direction of a houseful of nuns would suit you exactly. For my part, I want to preach to heathen and sinners, strong work, and I'm not anxious to spend my time absolving the imperfections of a community of saints; gilding the lily, so to speak.'

'I don't understand at all,' I said, quite bewildered.

'Shall I try to explain?' asked Stephen. 'Many of the earlier friars felt as Bernard does about the nuns—not our Father Dominic's companions, of course, but those who followed directly after. So, about six or seven years ago, they asked for and obtained a Bull removing all convents of our nuns from the jurisdiction of the Master General, and giving them to the care of the bishops. The nuns were both distressed and angry and never ceased pointing out, what was perfectly true, that the nuns had been given into the care of the friars by our Father himself. You know what women are when they have set their minds on a thing and are determined to get it? They managed to bring many of the friars round to their point of view. So only three years after the Bull removing them from the jurisdiction of the Order, at the Chapter at Buda, the Pope was asked and consented to give the friars the right to consider the requests of individual convents to return to the jurisdiction of the Master General. Now you can understand why Bernard said that the king had chosen the right moment to give us St Mary's. The request to be under the Order was made and granted before the monastery was handed over to the Master General at all and so the nuns have always belonged to us. Everywhere, more and more convents are asking to return to our jurisdiction.'

'And so, eventually, all will be as it was in the beginning,' added Bernard, 'and, willy nilly, we shall be doing work which is more proper to monks than to preaching friars.'

'And some of the nuns will be unfortunate enough perhaps to come under your care,' laughed Stephen and, turning to me, added, 'Can't you see him preaching hell fire to an audience of innocents who have never in their lives committed a mortal sin?'

'Don't be too certain of the innocence,' laughed Bernard in his turn, 'and in any case 'twill do them no harm. At any rate you must own that the king, not the nuns, was responsible in this case.

'How was he responsible?' I asked.

'The answer to that question is simple enough for even me to deal with,' said Bernard. 'Sister Margaret is the king's child. She was vowed to God before her birth, when Hungary, and the royal family as well, seemed doomed to come to a violent end at the hands of the Tartars. The king, the queen, and Stephen, the only child left alive, had been driven on to Trau, an island off Spalato, they were cut off from the mainland by Batu and his army, and the only way of escape left was to drown in the sea. God heard their prayers and accepted their vow. For some reason I know nothing about, the Tartars suddenly turned tail and marched back into Asia. When Margaret was four years old, her parents fulfilled their vow and sent her to our nuns at Veszprim; and by the time she was ten, the king had built a fine monastery, St Mary of the Isle, for her on the Isle of Hares. At the General Chapter, he gave it to Master Humbert. And he stipulated at the same time that it should be under the jurisdiction of the Order.'

'And you must own that our nuns are a fine lot of women and that the king's daughter is the best of them all.'

'Oh, I'll agree that Sister Margaret is as good as you like, but there are others. Sister Helena is a great soul, and half a dozen more that I could mention.'

'But they don't come up to Sister Margaret. Think of what she's done. Do you know, Thomas, that the king has tried above once to have her dispensed from her vows so that she could make a great political marriage? It's odd that he has forgotten that it is he, not she, who vowed her to God. Now nothing that either parent can say or do will make Margaret consent to give up the religious life.'

'Well, well!' remarked Bernard with a shrug. 'Though I am willing to grant that Margaret is very holy, I also find her very dirty. However, in less than an hour Thomas will be able to see and judge for himself. I wonder what he'll make of it all.'

We walked on in silence for a few minutes and then another matter which had interested me came into my mind. 'Why did the Cumans consider themselves so badly treated in the Tartar invasion?' I asked.

Both my companions burst out laughing.

'What a man you are for asking questions,' chuckled Stephen at last. 'And what is more, their subject matter is so unexpected and their range so wide.' He did not know, of course, that I had had the whole winter to store up such problems without seeing much prospect of having them solved.

'I'll leave Bernard to answer that question,' added Stephen.

'It was like this,' began my other companion promptly. 'When the Tartars came in '42, forty thousand Cumans from the east, with Kuthan, their king, begged for shelter in Hungary. They agreed to be baptized, and Bela allowed them to settle in the Thaiss valley. But the Magyar nobility were very angry. Fredrick, Duke of Austria, sympathized with their grievance and, under pretext of helping Hungary, against the Tartars, joined the nobles in massacring Kuthan and as many of his followers as they could. That was as far as his assistance went; to make things more impossible for Bela. Naturally the rest of the Cumans were so angry that, while one band made its way, a bloody way, out of Hungary, the others joined the Tartars who were besieging Pesth. Since the Tartars left the country there has been a kind of patched up friendliness. Because the king has always been partial to them he has allowed them to settle here; but the Cumans have not forgotten, and the Magyars don't like their presence, they feel that it is not safe to have them in the interior of the country. Then Prince Stephen is constantly with them and that does not add to the general sense of security. I can assure you that Hungary is an uneasy place to live in.'

By this time we had reached the bridge which crossed the Danube to the Isle of Hares, an islet quite close to the mainland. The monastery buildings were large and handsome and there was a fine church. On the far side were meadows with cattle and sheep and fields of upspringing grain; in all a very good estate.

As we reached the bridge Father Marcellus drove up. I said goodbye and thanked my two companions. Then I climbed up beside the provincial, and we drove across the bridge.

CHAPTER XVII

Why We Spent the Night at St Mary's Priory

As we drove across the bridge Father Provincial asked me whether I knew anything about the community at St Mary's.

'I knew nothing until today,' I answered. 'But I have been asking the brothers who brought me here, and I understand that they are very good, very austere and that many of them are exceptionally holy; but that the two most remarkable are Sister Margaret and Sister Helena.'

'Sister Helena?' The provincial raised his eyebrows. 'I should hardly have singled her out above many others.' He paused a second and then added, 'Oh, I know what has happened; they have confused two Sister Helenas. The Countess of Olympiade and Sister Helena Serrenj. The Olympiade remained behind at Veszprim. I'll tell you about her and something about Sister Margaret when we have the opportunity. She was Sister Margaret's Mistress when the little Princess entered at Veszprim, but she did not come with her to St Mary's. The Sister Helena here is a much younger woman.'

By this time we were in the monastery courtyard and Father Marcellus, giving the reins to an old serving-man, climbed out of the cart and led the way to the great door. It was opened at our knock by a middle-aged serving-woman, who led us through long echoing corridors to a room facing on the river. Near the door were a few seats and in the middle of the room a kind of table stretched from one wall to that opposite, so that no one could pass it. This was topped by a wooden grille taller than a man. There were wooden benches on the far side of it.

We waited in silence for a few minutes and I was beginning to feel thoroughly uncomfortable, when a door on the far side opened and a single nun came through. She was dressed exactly as we are except that, instead of a capuce, she wore a veil.

Father Marcellus greeted her as Mother Prioress and then introduced me as Thomas the Englishman, abroad to study. We spoke together for a few minutes and the prioress—Mother Catherine was her name—asked me a question or two about where I had come from and then she said:

'The sisters will like to hear all you have to tell them, brother, but Father Provincial sent word that he was coming to give us a conference. If you will begin by that, Father Provincial, the community will like to see you afterwards to hear all the news. Then, if you can spend the night here...'

The provincial interrupted: 'I'm sorry, Mother, but that is quite impossible; I have a quantity of work waiting for me at Buda, and I only managed this by breaking my journey.'

'What bad news! The Sisters will be very much disappointed, for it's so long since we saw you. However, we must make the best of a bad job. The maid will bring you both bread and wine, and we shall be ready in ten minutes.'

As she spoke the middle-aged woman came into the room with bread, cheese and a flagon of wine. As soon as we had finished the meal the provincial left me, and the woman came in again to know if I would care to see the altar furniture that King Bela had given to the monastery when he had handed it over to Master Humbert. The sacristan had given it to her to show me and so, for the moment, it was outside the enclosure.

She took me into a small room which, I suppose, adjoined the sacristy, and there she showed me two wonderful candlesticks made of jasper; a chalice and a paten, two palms in length and farther more in breadth, made of gold ornamented with large single pearls and decorated with inlay in various rich colors. There were copes richly embroidered with gold and gems; on the orfry was an image of the crucifix made of large pearls interspersed with smaller ones. I have never seen more beautiful things of their kind.

After I had examined these treasures at my leisure, I left the serving woman and strolled down the corridor to the entrance. I stood there for a while watching the sun make patterns on the water, admiring the towers of Buda on one bank and those of Pesth on the other, and thinking what a lovely place it was that King Bela had chosen for his daughter's monastery. Then I walked across the courtyard to the river bank. What trouble would be caused, I thought, if the Danube were to overflow, for the bank here was not more than an ell in height above the water, and the monastery was very close and on level ground. I suppose I must have been examining it very carefully, for presently I heard a voice:

'It has only overflowed once in a lifetime.' I looked up to see an elderly man mooring a skiff to the little jetty and coming ashore.

'How did you know what I was thinking of?' I asked. He laughed and told me that he was the farm bailiff of the monastery, and what I had been thinking of was only too obvious.

I have already mentioned that I had been studying Magyar during the winter, and to my great satisfaction I found that I understood enough to gather the gist of what the old man was saying, even though his speech was uneducated. I hoped to learn something about the nuns, but, curiously enough, he could speak about little except Father Marcellus. Apparently, the provincial had a tremendous reputation for sanctity among the Hungarians. The man spoke at length of his zeal, his charity, his gift for preaching, and of the efficacy of his prayers. He said that his care for the nuns was wonderful and their reverence for him unbounded.

At last I managed to bring him to the subject of the nuns. He had been with them ever since they came to St Mary's, he said, and he had been at Veszprim for some time before that. In fact he had been in charge of their removal from the mother convent; it had been a curious procession, he remarked, across country with carts of furnishings and carts of nuns. Their numbers at St Mary's were increasing rapidly; he knew this because of the constant increasing supplies of food that he had to bring in to them.

The original community had numbered ten. The prioress was that Sister Catherine who had given Sister Margaret her first lessons in Latin. Then there had been Sister Margaret herself, for whom the monastery had been built, and Sisters Eliana, Agatha, Alexandrine, Benedict, Cecilia, and Helen. Besides Margaret there had been two novices: Elizabeth, the foster sister of the princess, and Judith. All were now professed nuns.

Sister Margaret's position in the house? Oh, she held no office or position whatsoever. She made herself the servant of the rest and no one could prevent her. She looked after the sick sisters; no job that for anyone who was squeamish. More than that, she looked after the sick servants and farm hands, and cleaned their huts for them. And as for herself? Why, to look at her, you would think she was just nobody. And she a royal princess!

At this moment I caught sight of Father Provincial beckoning to me from the doorway.

'Our sisters are waiting for us in the guest room,' he said, and he led the way back to the room where we had seen the prioress. I followed him in and, as he moved aside from the doorway, I got my first glimpse of what was awaiting me, and it was all I could do not to turn tail and run away again as quickly as possible.

The far side of the room, beyond the grille, looked to me to be simply packed with women. There they sat, row on row of them on the wooden benches, for all the world like peas in a pod; white veils, black veils, white scapulars, black scapulars, each in their own lines. It was dreadful. I would far sooner have faced a den of lions.

However, English Thomas could hardly disgrace his nation by running away, so I took a deep breath, stared hard at the floor and made the best of my way to the seat placed for me close to the counter beside Father Marcellus. Then I kept my eyes fixed on my feet, for I did not dare look up and face those rows of nuns on the far side of the counter.

From the other side, however, came the sound of pleasant, cheerful voices. The nuns were bombarding the provincial with questions which he was doing his best to answer. After a minute or two I began to gather my wits together sufficiently to understand something of what was being said. The provincial was being questioned minutely about every detail of his journeys. Then the inquisition was turned on to the larger range of the Order in general, and of this or that province in particular. The nuns seemed to have a much more detailed knowledge of our affairs that I had ever had.

Presently, as no one took any notice of me, I summoned sufficient courage to look around. The nuns had cheerful intelligent faces, not nearly so grim and awe inspiring as I had expected. If the sanctity of these women awed the provincial, it was, nevertheless, a gay, gentle sanctity. Some did look rather severe, it is true, but these were in the minority. As a whole I found them reassuring.

They were all so intent on what Father Marcellus was saying, that I began cautiously to scrutinize those round me, wondering which was Princess Margaret; but I could make no guess. Presently, far to the back of the room, I espied one sitting a little apart from the others; she was a dirty, untidy looking little object, in a patched habit, with shoes gaping at the seams. What a pity, I thought to myself, that they let anyone get into such a dirty, untidy state; for she was in painful contrast to the rest who, though dressed for the most part in old habits, were clean and tidy.

At this moment, however, the sisters, seeing I suppose that I had lifted my head and was looking round, began to question me about England and my journey to Poland and Silesia and what I had seen there. They asked a number of questions about Jakato, and whether I had seen Father Sadoc. In short, it was a regular cross-examination, but they were so gay and friendly that I really did not mind it, and in the effort of trying to understand and answer in a mixture of Latin and Magyar, I forgot all about the little sister sitting alone at the far end of the room.

Presently the provincial turned to me.

'Thomas,' he said, 'it is time we were going. Go out and tell the stable man to put the horse in the cart and let me know as soon as it is ready. We must get back before nightfall.'

There was quite a clamor from the other side of the grille.

'Surely, you're going to stay over night, Father.'

'We were counting on your giving us another conference in the morning.'

'We have not seen you for months, surely you can stay a little longer now you are here.' And so on. The provincial shook his head.

'I'm sorry, sisters, but I must get home to work, for I am busy. Another time, I promise; but not now. Go, Thomas.'

As I left the room I glanced round at the disappointed faces of the nuns. The little blackamoor at the back of the room had her eyes shut and her lips were moving; but her face expressed—just nothing.

I went into the yard and the horse was brought out at once. But when we began to put him in the shafts, we noticed something.

'Look!' we both cried together. 'The axle is broken.' And, sure enough, it was snapped in two and quite unusable; a job for a wheelwright, and one that would take a considerable time by the look of things; for I used to know something about carts.

'How has this happened?' I asked angrily.

'Reverend Father, I don't know. No one has been near the cart, or even in the yard since it was brought in here.'

'But some one must have broken it, or rather, sawed it. It couldn't have broken itself like that.' I was furious, for it was a clean break cut right across. So it could not have been the result of accident or wear and tear.

'I have not left the yard all afternoon, sir, and no one has been in. It would take a couple of men with a saw to make such a break as that.'

'No need to tell me that, man, I'm not a fool.'

The bailiff came in at this minute and, seeing what had happened, began to question the man; but he could not move him. No one had been in the yard and no one had touched the cart. At last we looked at each other and shrugged our shoulders.

'The cart can't be used as it is,' said the bailiff. 'It is too late to do anything tonight. I'll send for the wright first thing in the morning.'

I went back to the guest room. As I came in, the provincial rose. 'Ready?' he asked.

I shook my head. 'The axle of the wheel is smashed, a clean cut across; no one knows by whom. The bailiff says he will send for the wright in the morning, but that it will be at least a day's work.'

The provincial shrugged his shoulders. Somehow he did not seem so surprised or angry as I had expected.

'So be it,' he said. 'We must stay the night then, whether we will or no. I'll give you, sisters, the conference you ask for in the morning. But,' and I thought he looked meaningly towards the far end of the room, 'there must be no mistake about it; the cart must be mended and I must leave here tomorrow morning.'

I glanced at him, smiling to myself. *If you imagine that any orders can mend that cart by tomorrow morning, you are mistaken,* I thought.

Chapter XVIII

Of Sister Helena Olympiade and of How We Left the Isle of Hares

We said Compline and afterwards the night Office in the big echoing church, while the sisters in the choir beyond the screen were saying theirs. I had never before heard women singing and chanting and their rendering of what I was accustomed to hear sung in men's deep voices struck me as something almost unearthly. To listen to the treble voices twining themselves round in the spaces of the choir and losing themselves in the heights of the roof gave me the impression of the singing of disembodied spirits rather than that of human beings; those very nuns I had heard laughing and talking only a few hours previously.

Before Compline we had a meal and during it I tried to find out more about Sister Margaret, where she was seated in the guest room and what she was like to look at. The provincial was not very communicative on that subject. I learnt that she had been sitting at the back of the room, but I could not place her at all. Father

Marcellus said very little more; she was a good little soul, was all he told me, humble and prayerful. But that might be said with equal truth of a number of religious. It was not until afterwards that I realized that, being her confessor and director, he was obliged to be very circumspect in speaking of her.

About Sister Helena, the Countess of Olympiade and a widow, he was much more communicative. Sister Helena had been Sister Margaret's foster-mother. She had seen most of her own children die during the Tartar invasion, and when, at the age of three and a half, the little princess had entered the Dominican monastery at Veszprim, famous for its strict observance, her foster mother had gone with her.

Being a grown woman, while Margaret was only a baby, Helena's novitiate was ended before the latter's had begun; and so, when the child had reached the age of reason Sister Helena was made her novice mistress. She trained the young novice most carefully in observance and in all the duties of the religious life. When Margaret was sent to her father's foundation at St Mary, Sister Helena had remained behind. Probably it was considered best that the young nun should not be too dependent on her.

With regard to Sister Helena, all spoke of her sanctity and there were many reports of preternatural occurrences. Whether these were true or not the provincial could not say. As I was only staying for a time in Hungary and did not belong to the province, he said that he did not mind repeating some of these reports to me, for he was sure that I would be very discreet. But as far as the province was concerned, both friars and nuns were discouraged from talking of the matter. No good purpose could be served; in fact, it might very well lead to mischief.

It was said that Sister Helena carried some of the marks of the stigmata; to wit, on her hands and on her right side. She had been praying in the church on the feast of our Father St Francis, when some of the sisters heard her cry out and, on running to the choir, they found her kneeling in ecstasy, while over her head hovered a gold ring surrounding a white lily. They distinctly heard Helena say: 'I beseech thee, most sweet Jesus, not to let this happen to me.' Then, after a moment's pause: 'But, if it must be so, then grant me, I pray, that nothing may be seen.' Afterwards, her prioress learnt that she had then received the wound of the nail on her right hand.

Often the sisters find her raised above the ground in ecstasy. Sometimes, while she is in ecstasy, the air is filled with heavenly melody, and she is heard talking with saints who seem to have appeared to her. More than once, the figure from a crucifix has been seen to leave its place and descend into her arms or rest between her hands.

Once during the night when she was praying, the bronze image left the cross on which it hung and came down into Helena's arms. The community heard the heavy thud of her fall and hurried to her, to find her lying motionless and inert on the ground, clasping the figure which was detached from the cross. The sisters tried to move the heavy figure and raise her up, but they found this impossible. However, about midday following, her senses returned to her, she rose and herself put back the figure on the cross from whence it had come.

She had a great devotion to the Holy Eucharist and, above once, when her confessor had refused to allow her to receive the Blessed Sacrament, our Savior himself had given her Holy Communion. She was reputed, so the provincial said, to have the gift of healing.

He ended like this: 'I am telling you, Thomas, the common talk about Sister Helena. For my part, I offer no opinion either way. In preternatural matters curiosity is quickly roused, the imagination stirred, and it is easy to be credulous. One cannot be too careful in reserving one's judgment until the Church declares either for or against, or decides that the matter under judgment is insufficiently proven. So I advise you to keep an open mind.'

Next morning after saying Mass, which I served, the provincial preached the sermon which he had promised. Seated as I was in the secular church, with the preacher's back to me, I could understand very little of what was said. At the conclusion, however, I heard him say this very distinctly:

'You have forced me to do your will, Sister; now you must give me back my cart.'

I wondered who on earth he was talking to and what he could mean by what he was saying; nor was I any less amazed, when I met him outside the church door and he told me to go at once and tell the ostler to put the horse in the cart without delay. After that I could come back to my breakfast, for we were starting immediately.

'But, Father,' I expostulated, 'don't you remember that the cart is unusable. The axle is broken and it will take at least a day to mend it.'

The provincial grinned, yes actually grinned. 'Nevertheless, do as I tell you,' he replied; and I went feeling a perfect fool.

I went into the yard to find the old man washing down the cart and when I got near enough, I could see that the axle was whole and entire without the slightest sign of a break. I need not say that I was surprised. So the provincial had known all along that the bailiff was going to fetch the wright and that they would spend the night mending it.

'My faith!' I cried. 'So the bailiff has had the cart mended after all. You must have been up all night. And, even so, I don't understand how you have finished the work so soon.'

The old man looked up from his work. 'Found it mended when I came down this morning, sir,' was his laconic reply; and as he turned to his work again, he added something between his teeth which sounded like: 'Not the first time it's happened, neither.'

I hurried back to the house and burst in on the provincial beginning his breakfast. 'The cart has been mended,' I cried, just as he raised his cup of wine to his lips, 'though how it has been done in the time I can't imagine.'

Father Marcellus put down his cup. 'I thought you would find it mended, Thomas,' was all he vouchsafed in reply.

As soon as I reached the priory in Buda I went in search of Brother Bernard. 'Bernard,' I said, 'I never discovered which was Sister Margaret. The provincial said she was there, but did not give me much help in finding out which was she.'

Bernard grinned: 'Did you happen to notice a shabby, dirty little sister sitting by herself at the back of the room? Well, that was Princess Margaret of Hungary.'

'Oh!' I gasped as the picture of the little blackamoor passed through my mind. I said no more. I could not.

CHAPTER XIX

How I returned to Kracow

My return to Poland was supposed to be made in early summer, and I was beginning to think that arrangements for the journey were never to be begun even. May and June passed and nothing was said about it. For some weeks the provincial was anxious, because one of the senior fathers, Augustine by name, had left Buda on a short preaching expedition in the first week of June; he should have returned early in July, but nothing had been heard of him and, as I had been told often enough, many tribes of Cumans were treacherous.

One evening towards the end of the month of July, the provincial sent for me.

'Thomas,' he said, 'I have been waiting for a good opportunity to send you to Kracow and now I think that I have one. The leader of a caravan of merchants came to see me this morning and he tells me that their party is setting out in two days from now. Most of the party are bound for Kiev, but a few are separating from the rest and making for Kracow where they have business. You will go with these. Fathers John and Dominic will go with the caravan as far as the mountains, and they will preach to the people they may meet. On their return they will follow up what they have done while they were with the caravan.'

I made the *Venia* and went out to find my companions. I was really pleased to be leaving Hungary; I had found it an uncomfortable place, and I had made several disconcerting discoveries there. I was fond of Poland. The two young men, my companions, were in great spirits. It was the first time they had been on mission except as the companions of a senior friar. They told me that we were going by road for the first part of the way, at least, and that they were anticipating work in plenty. For my own part, I was delighted to be able to see for myself how the friars managed to preach to the barbarians, specially if they did not know the language. In England even the roughest peasants, through markets and fairs, had some contact with the towns and nearly all spoke a dialect in which one could make oneself understood.

Now I am not going to attempt to describe our journey. As a matter of fact I travelled from day to day not troubling about the route and, except for the general features, paying little attention to the road by which we were travelling. Besides, what happened on the evening before we separated made such a vivid impression on my imagination as to dwarf everything else. The caravan was quite a large one and the merchants a pleasant set of men. There were four of five wagons drawn by pairs of horses, beside pack animals loaded with bales; and we rode with the merchants both before and behind the wagons. They were all armed. Being so large a party we travelled by the regular trade routes which were not particularly interesting.

At nightfall we halted at some open spot—there were regular camping places at intervals along the road. The wagons were set in the centre, the horses were loosed, fed and hobbled, and then tents were set up for the elder men and those who preferred shelter. Fires were made and a good hot meal cooked, after which we settled to sleep; my companions and I generally under the open sky. Next morning, before starting, we had another hot meal and then there was no more to eat or drink until evening. There was a halt and siesta at midday in the heat, but we just rested quietly where we were with everything in readiness to start immediately. The merchants, of course, spoke lingua franca, and when we halted at night would tell us of their adventures; very interesting, but not always very credible.

It was the friars' work which attracted me most. While the caravan was setting up camp for the night, rough, wild looking men and women would creep up to the outskirts and stand and stare. Then the two friars would begin to make their way slowly towards them. It reminded me forcibly of rounding up sheep on my grandfather's farm on the hills because, as they advanced, the strangers would withdraw gradually into the shelter of the trees or brushwood. Then, when the friars stood still, our visitors would begin to creep towards them.

At length the friars, and one of the merchant band who used to offer to accompany them to act as interpreter, would make a last halt and from all sides the strangers would advance slowly until they had made a circle around the three. The friars would proceed to welcome their visitors in every dialect of which they had any knowledge; and if they failed to make themselves understood, their companion would make trial.

If, at last, some common medium of speech was found, the friars would proceed to give a very simple instruction on God the Creator and Redeemer, would teach the strangers a very short prayer, often no more than the sign of the cross, and then would arrange to meet them again on a given day of the moon on their return journey. John and Dominic were only making a ten day march with us. Then they were to go back and, as they retraced their steps, being alone, they could make a stay of a week or ten days at each halting place.

It was very interesting to watch what the friars did when they could find no language in which to make themselves understood. They carried with them two or three pictures painted on wood. I remember one of heaven which struck me as being very crude. There was God on a throne and angels and souls of the just; and another, even more crude, of hell and the torments of the damned, while set round as a kind of frame were small pictures of sinners and their grievous sins. The friars would produce the picture of heaven first; point to the representation of God, then to the sky above and the world around and to each one of those watching. Then they would point to the just in their robes of glory. Next they would bring forward the picture of hell and show the sinners and their punishment.

They told me afterwards that they had no idea how much had been understood, but that, on their return journey, they could generally find one or more in another neighborhood who could speak the language a little, and they would persuade these to accompany them. They could not gauge, of course, what the interpreters made of the translations of the instructions; they feared at times that what reached the catechumens was something peculiar, but it was the best they could do for them. I learnt that these mountain tribes were Cumans.

Then there came an evening when I was told that on the following day the caravan was going to break up. The friars would turn on their tracks and make for home. I was going on horseback with three merchants, their bales would be strapped on pack horses. The main body, with the wagons, was going on to Kiev.

I was sorry; for John and Dominic had been very companionable, they had explained to me all that they were able; on one occasion they had even allowed me to take the instruction, but I cannot say that I made much of it. The people were so different to any that I had been accustomed to that I did not seem able to make contact of my mind with theirs. I preferred the children who often followed their elders, and I used to stand on the outskirts of the crowd and coax them to come to me. Though they were indescribably dirty and verminous, I felt more at home among them, even if I did little but play with them.

This evening, the one before we parted, no strangers came to the camp, an unusual occurrence but one which the merchants seemed to expect there. So, after supper, we three went off into the rough country on the outskirts of the camp. The merchants shouted to us to be very careful and not to wander too far as this was a hostile neighborhood; the folk being pagans who hated Christianity and were not to be trusted. We promised not to go far and made for a thicket on a knoll not far off, so that a cry would bring help at once.

My companions were very lighthearted; they were looking forward to travelling alone and going to the villages of the people they had met on the outward journey. I too was feeling gay, I am afraid chiefly because my first two years of exile were over and I could begin to think of home again. I made a very poor figure as a friar preacher in those days; I am not much better now.

We reached the small wood which had a bridle path running through it. We decided to follow this to the other side and then return. I remember how John was telling us that once he had been out on mission with a friar, many years his senior and inclined to be stout. They reached a Cuman encampment where the welcome was anything but cordial. They were feeling uncomfortable about their reception, wondering what was going to happen next and whether they would be allowed to preach, when suddenly an old man hobbled out from a seat on a bale of hay near the fire and seized the elder friar in his arms, shouting some version of his name. This greeting was so unexpected and the friar so astonished that, between the sudden impact of the two heavy bodies, and the old man being so unsteady on his feet, they had both fallen backward into a pile of brushwood set ready for making up the camp fires.

The other Cumans were delighted, roared with laughter and, picking the two out of the brushwood, carried them off to one of the fires where a cauldron was hanging. There the friars shared in an enormous but not very savory meal; and from that moment their visit was a complete success.

Then, without warning, we suddenly came on it.

A body hung between two trees by the side of the path. The man had been dead for several days, for carrion crows had already been busy with the body and the stench, when the breeze blew our way, was sickening. A few tattered rags still hung from what had once been the shoulders, and after a minute we realized that those rags had belonged to a Preacher's habit; there were white tatters and black ones and by some miracle the scapular, almost intact, covered the body. The arms were stretched out, tied by ropes to the branches of two trees, the lower part hung loose; and there it danced and dangled in the wind, a grotesque horror.

With a gasp my companions stopped dead and stared. What I did I do not know.

'It is Augustine,' one of them whispered at last.

'He's been tortured to death,' murmured the other.

'For preaching,' said the first in what was a sigh.

Then, quite suddenly, they straightened themselves, pulled their capuces over their heads, crossed their hands under their scapulars, faced chorally and sang the *Te Deum* right through. And the thing that had once been a man danced and dangled in the wind as they sang. A horrible semblance to a crucifixion. And this was martyrdom.

Afterwards, we found a cavity between two rocks, and somehow, by using a saw, we got the body down. John ran back to the camp for a saw, but he did not tell the merchants what we had discovered. We lowered the body into the cavity we had found, and made all secure by rolling in stones and earth until it was all filled in. And the sweet evening air was polluted by the smell.

It was growing dark by the time we had finished, but before going back we knelt and said a *De Profundis* for the soul of Father Augustine. Dominic suggested this, for he said that, though we might hope that, as a martyr, he had gone straight to God, yet, hung up as he was, he might have been some time dying and his agony would certainly have been very great. We had only found his remains and no one could tell with complete certainty how and when he had died. The same had happened to Father Paul and many others of our brethren in Hungary. The two had not known him well for he was much their senior in age and religion, but they knew that the provincial and the senior fathers had thought very highly of him.

We walked back quickly in the dusk and my companions, who had recovered quickly, I thought, from the shock of our find, were talking cheerfully together. Presently John turned to me.

'You are very silent, Thomas,' he said.

'Sights like that make one think,' I replied. Then I said: 'Suppose the same thing should happen to us?' I did not really mean that: not death or torture, but the disgrace. Being hung like vermin, left to dangle on a tree because one was not worth the labor of taking down. The other two could not follow my thought. Why should they?

'Suppose the same thing should happen to us, what then?' asked John, quite surprised. 'Isn't that why we entered the Order? I pray that if and when my turn comes, as it probably will, I have the grace to stand up with a joyful heart to whatever they may do to me.'

I made no answer and presently Dominic chimed in: 'Surely death is a thing that we all see often enough and in every form. You must have seen executions and quarters hung on city gates, even if you have never been in a battle?'

'It isn't death,' I answered and could say no more. How could I explain to those lads that to see and read of such shameful rewards for the dedication of a life to God and souls was the thing that shocked me. I knew I could never make them understand.

By this time we had reached the camp and John went to report to the head merchant what we had found. He nodded his head and did not seem much surprised. 'I told you the neighborhood was dangerous,' was all that he said. But, all the same, he made arrangements to set a guard for the whole night and advised all his companions to have weapons to hand, ready to use at a moment's notice.

Then we lay down, the three of us near each other, and wrapped our cappas about us; for though the days are hot, the nights are often extremely cold. From the sound of their deep breathing I concluded that my companions were soon asleep, they were two brave men; but I lay awake, growing more wakeful as the night wore on.

Over and over again I remembered John's remark, 'Isn't that why we entered the Order', asking myself if I had entered in the expectation of a death like Father Augustine's; and I could not find it in my heart to answer: yes. I had entered prepared for martyrdom certainly. But the martyrdom of my imagination had been a public one: that of Stephen, stoned to death; of Sebastian pierced with arrows; of being torn to pieces by wild beasts in the area; of being tortured in public. But to be hung there to die alone, just like some noxious beast or bird of prey! The shame; the disgrace; the hours alone; left there in contempt, deprived even of the stimulus of enemies exalting around one!

I remembered Kazemierz and his Lady Truth. I remembered my ideal of our Savior, the young Hero, dying for us on high, above even our compassion. That was the Master's death; and then: what I had seen that evening; a rotting corpse, dangling and swinging just clear of the ground. Was that what God the Hero asked of his followers? I had learnt so much of similar rewards. There was Anzelinus with his companions standing for the livelong day in the Tartar camp, objects of scorn and mockery of the barbarians. And then, after all they had patiently suffered, they were to trudge home, their mission a failure. There was little Margaret, who had given up a great position and a noble marriage for his sake, sitting alone, dirty and unkempt, at the far end of the room, apart from the community whose princess she was. There was Augustine, hanging alone, without even the jeers of his enemies for sorry companionship.

At last I could endure it no more. It was impossible to lie there as still as might be for fear of waking my companions—to lie there and think; so I rose very quietly and slipped away to the edge of the encampment, where I could walk up and down without fear of disturbing anyone.

I tried to say my Rosary. It was useless. My soul was surrounded by a thick, black mist. I was groping in darkness to find my way, I did not know where. All that was left to me was to walk and walk.

With the first gleam of dawn, for daylight comes quickly so far south, I crept back to my place between my two companions and lay there until the camp was roused for a meal and departure. Afterwards we separated. I said goodbye to my companions, who were still in a cheerfully expectant frame of mind. After they had gone, I went to find the merchants with whom I was to travel to Poland.

Our journey was uneventful, and a week later we reached Kracow.

Chapter XX

How I spent the Last Winter of My Stay at Sandomierz

I was very sorry when I reached Kracow to find that my friend Albert had been sent to Paris to the University to study and teach; the natural thing for such a brilliant man to do and one which I had expected, but I missed him much all the same. There were quite a number of changes besides this, but the man whose loss I felt most of all was Father Hyacinth. When Jasek went to God, something very strong, gentle and reliable was taken away from the Polish Province, and one felt his absence everywhere.

In the darkness and trouble in which I found myself, I used often to go to his grave to pray, and I never left it without the conviction that somehow God would show me his will and that, in this showing, I should find the solution of my difficulties and light in the darkness of my trouble. But, wherever I went, I was accompanied by Anzelinus and his companions, Margaret silent and sitting apart, and Augustine swinging and dangling between the trees. And always, I was pursued by the question Is this the way in which God rewards faithful service?

One day early in September Father Provincial sent for me.

'How many languages can you speak?' he asked abruptly.

'I speak none but English and Latin really well,' I answered, 'but I am fairly fluent in French and German, I have a little Magyar and a smattering of Arabic. These two I picked up at Buda during the last year.'

The provincial considered this for a minute. 'Well, get your things together as quickly as possible and ask the vestiarius to give you a couple of new habits; yours are threadbare. I am sending you for the winter to the novitiate house at Sandomierz. You can take the first boat going that way. You will stay there until next spring. This time you are to teach, not to study for, when he returned here, Albert told us that you had gained your Lectorate at Oxford. When you reach the priory the prior, Father Sadoc, will tell you what to do. That should complete your education as far as we are concerned.' He smiled as he spoke, and I made the *Venia*. 'God go with you,' he said.

I collected my wallet and a couple of habits as I had been told and set off for the river front at once. I did not know whom I was to teach, or what I was to teach my pupils. I could do no more than my best, and that I was determined to do. There was one comfort. To be near that great lion, Father Sadoc, was bringing me in a way nearer to his friend Jasek.

The winter that I spent at Sandomierz was, in many respects, a happy experience. The burden of my troubles did not grow less, but by sheer hard work I could often escape from their most pressing weight. The more I saw of Prior Sadoc the more I realized what a wonderful man he was. As was inevitable, he was often away, but when he was at home, he seemed to fill the house with his own joy and enthusiasm. His discourses, in the daily Chapters he held when he was in residence, were full of instruction, and there were times when he would tell us all of the early days: of our Father Dominic, of Paul of Hungary and of our other early brethren. Though he was strict, he was also exceedingly kind.

I found my work very interesting. In the mornings the novices came to me in twos and threes and to the best of my ability I taught them the elements of German, French, English and Magyar, according as the novice master directed me. For the first year of the novitiate, they were set to study the rule, constitutions, ceremonial, and the religious life in general. To this was added a foreign language. Other studies were reserved until this preliminary year was past.

In the afternoon I took cursory lectures with the junior students. I gave courses in logic, scripture, science and the elements of philosophy, and for much of this I was indebted to my friend Albert. Of course my lectures were informal, more like talks and discussions, for the formal ones, the Masters' lectures, were given in the morning; my work really consisted in the clearing of difficulties and hearing repetitions. I enjoyed this contact with young, keen minds and strove, though vainly, to regain through them all my own young ideals.

It was a great relief to me to find that Kazemierz was wintering at Prague, teaching and studying there. Naturally I made enquiries about him and gathered that he was still living as a kind of troubadour friar; modeling his life on the romances of the minnesingers and worshipping his Lady Truth. The elder men were of the opinion that this was an unwise thing to do and, in reality, he had been sent to Prague because his influence was not considered good for the young men. When he returned in the following summer, he was to be sent out preaching. If preaching in the country places of Poland was much like what I had seen in Hungary, the devotee of Lady Truth would not make much impression on Kazemierz's hearers.

For my own part, I do not think that I could have borne to listen to him now that I had passed beyond idealism and romance, and was trying to grope my way to something which I knew to be very stark and real. I often thought of him and prayed for him and I hoped he did the same for me; but I was very glad that he was not at Sandomierz. He was due back just at the time when I returned to Kracow and so we never met.

The winter was very cold and the Vistula frozen, but I did not feel it like I had felt the winter of the previous year, and we had some good times skating on the frozen river. I was very sorry in many ways when May came and it was time to return, but at Kracow I was to prepare to return to England. I carried with me very happy memories of the community at Sandomierz, especially of the prior Sadoc.

CHAPTER XXI

How the Provincial Received News from Sandomierz

It was August before I at last sailed for England. During early summer there was much anxiety at Kracow, for the Scythians, barbarians belonging to the Tartar race, were making many raids into Poland, and each incursion had its tally of martyrs. Among many other places, we heard that they had destroyed the convent of the Poor Clares at Zanichodense, and that of the Cluniacs at Lystense, and had violated the nuns. The two principal chiefs were named Nogaria and Celebuga.

Later on we heard that a band was besieging Sandomierz but, as this was a fortified city, we had not much fear that the Scythians would get beyond the outer wall. Then rumors reached us that some Russians, who were with the enemy, had asked and obtained admission to the town in order to make terms for a truce. This was not reassuring, but we hoped for the best and prayed for those in danger.

At last one evening about a week later we heard that a messenger had arrived with a letter for the provincial.

The porter told us that the man was a scarecrow, half starved and utterly worn out. Bit by bit we learnt more. The messenger said that he had had the greatest difficulty in making his way from Sandomierz to Kracow for the whole countryside was infested with marauding bands of Tartars.

The evening that he left the city, the treacherous Russians had opened the gates to the Scythians outside. He had escaped by ways known to few even of the inhabitants, and everywhere the slaughter had been terrible. He would have stayed with the community, but he had been strictly charged to bring the provincial a letter written by the Subprior. He understood that the massacre at Sandomierz was not part of a regular campaign to subdue Poland, but one of the series of raids. In fact, he had seen that for himself, for, as he made his secret escape through the Scythian lines outside the city, he saw that there were none but fighting men; no women and no tents such as were always found when the Tartars were carrying out a planned campaign of subjugation. By the time that he reached Kracow, the devastated city would be, in all probability, deserted, and the raiders far away.

Later that same evening the provincial had us all summoned to the chapter room, where he read the subprior's letter which the messenger had brought.

'From our Priory of Saint Mary Magdalen at Sandomierz, in the hand of the very Reverend Father Provincial. Your Reverence will already have heard how this city is being besieged by the Scythians. In the ordinary course of events, the danger should not be great, but we hear that the Russians are in the gates making terms. Therefore I have been told to write an account of what has happened, and send it to you by a trustworthy messenger.

'Last night, when we had finished saying Matins and Lauds, according to custom, a novice went to the lectern to read the Martyrology for the following day. First in place among the notices, he saw written in letters of gold a new notice: "AT SANDOMIERZ THE PASSION OF FORTY-NINE HOLY MARTYRS".

'He was both frightened and in doubt whether or no to read what was written. But at last, remembering that we are enjoined to read what is before us just as it is written, he conquered his fear sufficiently to read in a trembling voice, the golden notice: "AT SANDOMIERZ THE PASSION OF FORTY NINE HOLY MARTYRS".

'You may understand how shocked we all were; the Prior looked stupefied and the rest whispered to one another, wondering if the novice had made it up as an ill-timed joke, or if, knowing him to be a young man of good and earnest purpose, the book contained a message for us. Presently Father Sadoc asked for the Martyrology. The novice brought it as he was told and the Prior saw the golden words for himself. He passed it to the friar next him and so on round the chapter room and, as it went from one to the other, the letters gradually disappeared beginning with Sandomierz. But all saw some part of it.

'Then the Prior held chapter and gave us an instruction: "My brothers," he said, "there is special meaning in the fact that these words have been show first

177

to innocent eyes. It is most certain that the Author of life and death is calling us to a happier life and a blessed immortality. If that be so, come, my brothers, let us run hot foot to the swords of the spoilers. What does it matter if the Scythians deprive us of life? Death is always waiting for us and we are surrounded by perishable things. On all sides we see danger and calamity. It belongs to us to make port on these waves. We must reach harbor with sails spread, and direct our course through the open way of death to the glory of eternal life. Now I beg of you to examine your consciences and, if you find your souls to be stained with sin, make a good Confession. After that, strengthen your souls with the most sweet Viaticum, for we are shortly to seek our heavenly kingdom. Thus adorned with sanctifying grace and ready for whatever may happen, prepare your necks for the sword. We must die, but let our death be a joyful one. For this one, let his rock of strength be the altar of God, for that one, Christ crucified, for another, the Mother of God, for yet another, the unbloody sacrifice of the altar. In patience must our fortitude be shown."

'Now we are waiting for our end with joy. Animated by the Prior's words, we are using what remains of life to prepare for the longed-for coming of God. It is wonderful to see men so quiet and self-contained, saying aloud as they go about the work of the day:

"O when will that desired time come when we shall leave earth for heaven."

"How happy we are!"

"How I long for the sword which will send my soul to heaven."

"Most sweet Jesus, hope of those who long for you!"

"O, Mary when?"

'Your Reverence will be happy to know that all have been to Confession and received Holy Communion by way of Viaticum.'

When the provincial had finished reading, he sat for a moment or two twisting the piece of parchment in his hands, then he spoke:

'I would ask you to pray for the community at Saint Mary Magdalen, but by this time they are either out of danger or, as this letter suggests, we ought to be praying to, not for, them. We have no news of the priory of Saint James, so please remember them. It is a time of danger for Poland and for all who live there. Let us pray for all Poles, and for ourselves also that, if our time should come we may have the grace to face death joyfully.'

He left the Chapter room and we followed. In the cloister outside a few words were spoken. Some envied the good fortune of the community at Saint Mary Magdalen, others wondered what had happened to our other priory of Saint James. The majority of the friars went straight into the church, and the rest soon followed them.

I slipped in at the back and knelt alone in a place a little apart, praying and thinking. I had only just left the priory, where all had been very kind to me. Each friar, from the prior down, passed through my memory, I could recall some little characteristic of most of them, and I prayed to, and for, each in turn. Then I remembered the novices whom I had taught. I could make a guess as to the reader of the Martyrology; only one would have behaved with such a mixture of timidity and simplicity. I made a special petition to him. Martyrdom such as theirs I could understand and, in a way, rejoice in, and I prayed that, if it was my lot to die for the Faith, my death might, by the mercy of God, be like this.

We all remained in the church until Matins and most of us kept vigil afterwards until Prime. When we went into the chapter room after Lauds for the Martyrology and Pretiosa, I was fanciful enough to wonder whether there might not be an announcement in letters of gold in our Martyrology; but, of course, everything passed as usual.

Early in the morning the provincial sent for me.

'I must make certain,' he said, 'of what has actually happened to the community at Saint Mary Magdalen's, so I am sending Father Nicholas to find out. I have been making enquiries and, for the moment it should be safe to travel by boat. I am sending two overland to find out what has happened to the community at Saint James. When the Scythians are raiding like this, it is quite possible for one quarter of the town to be destroyed and another untouched. What I am going to ask you is in no way an obedience. Would you like to be Father Nicholas' socius as you have so lately lived in the priory?'

For the moment I was taken aback for, though I had known that the provincial would send someone to ascertain the fate of the community, it had not entered my head that I, a stranger, would be one of the chosen ones. I did not know whether I wanted to go, I only knew that, as the opportunity had offered itself, I must go.

I took a deep breath and made the *Venia*. When I rose to my knees, the provincial was smiling at me. He gave me his blessing in silence, however, and still in silence I left the room and went in search of Father Nicholas.

I found him waiting in the cloister for me, a burly, middle-aged man, very self-contained and matter-of-fact; one of whom I had never made much. He also smiled when he saw me, and the whole expression of his face altered.

'Get your stick and bundle, Thomas,' was all that he said, 'for we must start at once.'

I hurried off to do as I was told, slipped into the church for a moment to pray at Jasek's grave. Then we left the priory and made the best of our way down to the wharf.

CHAPTER XXII

What We Found at Sandomierz

We travelled by boat to within a few miles of Sandomierz, and then we walked the rest of the way. We had been sent to find out the fate of the community at Saint Mary Magdalen's and so it was part of our obedience not to run into danger if it could be avoided. To travel by land was much less conspicuous and would give us a much better opportunity of entering the city unnoticed, suppose that Scythian bands were still in the neighborhood.

We found the gateway open and the gates torn clean off their hinges, but the walls and ramparts had suffered little damage. The enemy bands had stormed through the city like a great wind scattering and destroying everything in its track. The marauders had carried off whatever loot lay to hand and had then stormed themselves away again. We were somewhat surprised to notice how quickly they had come and gone.

There were dead strewn in the streets. Soldiers lay think round the gate which they had evidently defended as best they could when the Russians broke faith, overpowered the guard and opened the way to the Tartars. Like a band right across the city lay the track of devastation, but beyond this broad belt, buildings stood intact. People were finding their way back.

In the streets parties were collecting the dead and large pits were being dug outside the walls to serve as common graves. A group of Master Builders and artisans were examining the gateway, evidently preparing to rebuild it. The Poles are a brave and hardy nation.

We followed the storm track right through the city to our priory of Saint Mary Magdalen. That seemed to mark the end of the Tartar advance, for beyond, the roofs shone in the sunlight and there was a broad double track where the enemy had turned back.

From a distance the priory and church looked untouched but, as we came nearer, we saw that the entrances were doorless, church windows broken, furniture smashed to atoms and scattered all around. The silence over the whole place was profound.

We made our way through the rubble to the church. At first sight it was empty and the only sound of life anywhere was a jackdaw chattering high in the groining of the roof. We picked a path as best we could through the porch. The broken door waved backwards and forwards in the wind, under our feet the fragments of glass crackled. Inside, the nave looked as though struck by a whirlwind. We reached the transept and the choir, and stood for a moment horrified at the wreckage. Then we turned left towards the Lady Altar, and saw what we had been looking for.

There before the Lady Altar lay two rows of white figures, for it was after Easter and cappas are not worn. It was like the prostration which we make at the announcement of the Annunciation in the Martyrology before Lady Day.

Father Nicholas dropped on his knees and I knelt beside him. After a few moments he rose and went to the prostrate figures. They had been killed in haste by clean sword thrusts and so were not mutilated. We counted forty-eight.

'There were forty-nine in community,' I whispered; and my heart was sick with sorrow for the friar who had forgone this grace.

Very reverently, we turned them over one by one and carried them into the nave. And because I had lived among them so recently, Father Nicholas told me to name each as we turned the body over. Although they must have been dead for days, corruption had not touched them and their faces were radiant.

The missing friar was Kazemierz.

Presently, in the silence we heard a little sound, the tap-tapping of a stick and a halting footstep. We listened to it growing louder as its owner came towards the church porch. As we turned a little old man came into sight, very lame and leaning heavily on a stick. Nicholas went down to him and I followed.

'What do you want?' he asked in a low tone.

The old man lifted his bent head. 'I have come to pray to them,' he said. 'I was here.'

'Here, in the church when this happened?' Nicholas' whisper was so sharp as to be almost a hiss.

'Yes, sir, I was there in that corner behind that pillar. I saw it all. When I heard the barbarians break into the town, I came here to be with them. I wanted to die with them. But I am very lame, and by the time I got to the Lady Altar the Tartars had gone.'

'Can you tell us what happened?'

'I think so, sir.' Then in a horse whisper with many pauses the old man began his tale.

'We were uneasy all day, though we thought the Russians were our friends. But, as soon as it was dusk, they came out of their lodging in a body, overpowered the guard and opened the city gates. They say that the guard was killed to a man. I could hear the din of battle and hobbled in here. If the Tartars did not come this way I was safe; and if they did, what better could I do than die with the friars. The din kept growing louder, and by the time they came in to sing Compline, the screams of the wounded and dying and the shouts of the barbarians had grown terribly close; but the friars all looked so peaceful and happy. Indeed some of them looked gay.

'As they sang Compline, the noise was so terrible that, at times, it drowned the voices. They began the *Salve* Procession. Then, as they reached the Lady Altar and knelt down, the doors broke open with a crash and about twenty or so barbarians rushed in, dashed up to the kneeling community as they began to sing the *"Eia ergo, Advocata nostra"* and thrust them through the body with their javelins, twisting each man round in drawing out the point, so that they lay as you see them; for, of course, they were facing the altar. That is, they killed all but one who rushed away to the church tower as the doors broke down.

'They must have died at once, but—O my God!—the singing still went on—those dead men sang—they finished the *Salve*: "*Et Jesum, benedictum Fructum ventris tui, nobis post hoc exilium ostende.*" And shouting and yelling in fear, those barbarians turned and ran; and as they dashed down the church, pushing and jostling each other, they crashed over and broke seats and everything moveable in their flight. And still the singing went on.

'I had just pulled myself to my feet as they reached the church door, and the friar who had hidden himself came out to them saying: "I also am a Friar Preacher." And one of them struck him through with a sword as he passed. And they ran into the street calling to their companions to leave the place, for it was bewitched.

'And that—and that is all, sir. And why—O why was I not judged worthy to be one of them?' The old man broke down completely, and Father Nicholas began to talk to him, comforting him and telling him that he was left to tell us the story of what had happened to our brothers, for without him we should have known almost nothing. When the old man was a little consoled, Nicholas began to question him very gently, and I slipped away to find Kazemierz if I could; the man who made the forty-ninth friar.

As I went down the church again, for the old man had told his story standing close to the dead friars, I thought, with admiration, of the unconquerable courage of the Poles. I could not imagine any other race in the world whose dead men would have finished their song in praise of Our Lady.

By the pillar before the entrance to the tower I saw a pool of dried blood, and a smeared blood track leading round it to the tower. A wounded man must have dragged himself there on his belly, his mind set on something which was greater than the pains of death.

I turned the corner and came face to face with the terrible blood-stained crucifix, hanging just clear of the ground; the crucifix which had so shocked and offended me on my first visit to Sandomierz, nearly three years previously, that all winter I had not climbed the tower so that I need not pass it again. At its foot lay Kazemierz. Somehow, even in his death agony he had managed to twist himself over so that, lying on his back, he could look up at it. His open sightless eyes were fixed on the Crucified, and his dead lips were smiling. And I understood.

At this moment I heard Father Nicholas' voice calling my name softly. He wanted me to help him carry the bodies of our brothers out into the nave of the church and set them ready for burial. So I picked Kazemierz up in my arms and carried him out to be with the rest; the forty-ninth friar who had joined them just before it was too late.

I fetched cappas from the place where they were hung. I knew my way about so well. We lifted each of them, put on the cappa and lowered the capuce over the face. The old man had been just outside and had found four or five men who lived nearby. They dug a grave in the cloister garth, and we carried the bodies out and laid them there, sprinkling them with holy water.

As we lifted Sadoc last of all, I thought of how he and Jasek had met again in the courts of heaven, and what a joy the meeting had been to both.

It took us two days to complete the work, and on the morning of the third day, Father Nicholas and I both said Mass, for he had brought a few Altar Breads with him. The Blessed Sacrament was not in the church, for, as Father Sadoc had been prepared for the barbarians, all the Hosts had been consumed by the community as their Viaticum.

After Mass we set out on the return to Kracow.

The night before we left, I spent in vigil before the great crucifix near the tower. I had to sort my thoughts.

CHAPTER XXIII

What I Thought as I Knelt in Vigil before the Great Crucifix in the Church at Sandomierz

When it was dark and we had finished our work, I went to the bottom of the church and said the *Veni Creator* before the crucifix there. Kazemierz's blood stained the ground at its foot, and I knew that in death he had found what I had learnt without dying.

I thought of what had so greatly shocked me when I first saw that life-size, terrible, blood-stained Figure. Those who had carved it and hung it had not raised the Christ on high, as the young Hero, but had left him here, on our level almost, just as if he had been one of ourselves. Perhaps they were right and I had been wrong. Perhaps he intended to hang just like one of ourselves; Augustine on the bough of the tree, for instance.

He had said: 'When I shall be lifted up, I will draw all men to myself.' He did not say: 'When I shall be lifted on high,' nor did he promise: 'I shall raise all men up to myself.' So, perhaps the actual cross was not really raised much above the height of a tall man and he did actually hang there, among us, as one of ourselves.

If that were so, and there is no passage of scripture which denies it, then those who mocked and jeered at him could look right into his Face as they did so. He was alone, because the ring of soldiers around the cross would prevent his few friends from coming too close, but, though at a short distance away from him, his Mother and the Beloved Disciple were not so far below his level in height. His Mother could see every detail of his torn and bleeding Body. By lowering his eyes he could look into hers, raised up towards him.

He the God-Man was just one of us, and he died among us as one of us; as less than any of us.

Back into my memory came the chapter* in Isaias, one of the many bible passages we had to learn as students:

'Who has believed our report? And to whom is the arm of the lord revealed?

'And he shall grow up as a tender plant before him, and as a plant out of a thirsty ground. There is no beauty in him, nor comeliness; and we have seen him, and there is no sightliness that we should be desirous of him:

'Despised and the most abject of men, a man of sorrows and acquainted with infirmity: and his look is as it were hidden and despised. Whereupon we esteemed him not.

---

* Chapter 53

'Surely he hath borne our infirmities and carried our sorrows: and we have thought him as it were a leper, and as one struck by God and afflicted.

'And he was wounded for our iniquities; he was bruised for our sins. The chastisement of our peace was upon him; and by his bruises we were healed.

'All we like sheep have gone astray, everyone hath turned aside into his own way; and the Lord hath laid on him the iniquity of us all.

'He was offered because it was his own will and he opened not his mouth. He shall be led as a sheep for the slaughter and shall be dumb as a lamb before his shearer, and he shall not open his mouth.'

And so through the chapter which ends with these words: 'And he hath borne the sins of many and hath prayed for the transgressors.'

Then I looked at the image of the mangled Body. What followed in my mind was necessarily incomplete in form, but the general idea was there and remained with me, and I have studied it over and over again in these intervening years until I cannot really separate my thoughts during that vigil from their outcome. Therefore I can only write the formulated conclusions of what I then saw 'Through a glass in a dark manner.' (Cor: XIII 12). These are memories as I see them now.

There is no suffering, either of mind or body, we can endure that Christ has not already tasted to the full. He can say of all: 'I know from personal experience what this is like.' In the most perfect way he is our Brother. As a good Brother he shares everything with us, and pain and trouble shared loses half its sting in the sharing.

Again all that is represented to us by the image of the cross happened over twelve hundred years ago. Time is defined as movement and movement is proper to material beings only. Our bodies are subject to time; while he lived on earth Christ's Body was subject to time and movement. In so far as they are the form of our bodies, our souls, while in our bodies, are subject to time; but in themselves, as living incorporeal beings, they are not subject to the time factor.

And so the Sacrifice of the Mass is one and the same with that of the Cross. Each day we are present body and soul at one, two, three Masses according to the number we hear; but our souls, in so far as they are pure form, are present at the one, the unique Sacrifice of Calvary, where Christ, the Victim, is offered until the end of time. And, for this reason, each, several suffering of ours, whether mental or physical, is privileged and glorious, because, through being the members of the Body of which he is the Head, we have the honor of being—yes actually being—a part of the Passion of Christ.

Anzelinus and his companions, standing in the blazing sun, mocked and jeered at by the barbarians, were, so to speak, other Christs, as he stood in ignominy before the Jews and Roman soldiers. Then there was the friars' weary journey back, knowing all the time that their mission was a failure. When Christ died, his life's work was such a complete failure that only his Mother believed in him and in the triumphant accomplishment of his mission. Only she knew what he meant when he cried 'consummatum est.'

If little Margaret was shunned by her community and they let her know that they preferred her not to come too close to them; Margaret's Master was the most despised and abject of men—a worm and no man.

And Augustine dangling between those two trees? I never needed to follow that train of thought farther nor to make it more explicit.

I next considered the question of suffering and failure as per se, and not with respect to this or that particular person. As far as it concerns each one of us personally, it is our honor to be in the likeness of our Head. I looked up at the crucifix again and substituted the word 'Brother' for 'Head.' I could look steadily up at the crucifix now. If that was how he died he was completely one of ourselves.

But why did Christ choose disgrace and failure for himself? What I had learnt about this question in theology came to my help. First: Christ must suffer because such was the Divine decree. A second reason came nearer to the need of the moment. Sin is of infinite malice, not in itself because it is the act of finite creatures, who are incapable of any but finite actions; but, because sin is an offence against the infinite God, deliberate grievous sins have, as it were, infinite malice.

Therefore it was necessary for Christ to suffer, not so much to redeem us, for he could have done that by a word, as to make reparation to God for the insult offered to his infinite Majesty; and such reparation can only be made by a God-Man: God in his infinity, Man in that during his mortal life he was passible like ourselves.

If then it was necessary for Christ, the innocent One to suffer, the least that we, the guilty ones can do is to make reparation also, and offer our mite in union with his sufferings and the infinite merit of his sacred Passion.

In imagination I again saw the dead body of Kazemierz lying just where I was kneeling. At his journey's end, he had learnt what God's mercy was even now teaching me in the full vigor of life. He had learnt then that success or failure, praise or blame, joy or sorrow, all these count for nothing. The only thing that matters is the close following of Christ wherever he chooses to lead us. It is not asked of us to look up to unattainable heights, but to gaze out on him as our Way. If he is the Way then it is possible for each of us to come by him, to take up our cross daily and follow him.

I prostrated and said: 'Jesus Christ, my hands are in yours I am your man, to do your Will to my life's end.'

It was the act of homage I had already paid at my profession. But what we do then, in our youth, is done by the grace of God almost blindfold; we accept an unknown future. Later, when one has sampled religious life in all its difficulties, any renewal of our vows is made with open eyes; we know what we are doing and we make an offering which embraces everything and is explicit.

I stayed where I was at the foot of the cross until morning. After I had given my tiny offering to God, he gave to me; and his infinite giving is only finite because our measure of receiving it is finite.

CHAPTER XXIV

I Leave Poland

Father Nicholas and I set out from Sandomierz early in the morning and our return to Kracow was uneventful. It was evening of the third day when we reached the priory tired and hungry. At the door we met the procurator who told us he had received orders from Father Provincial that, as soon as we returned, we were to have a good meal in the infirmary refectory, and then, when we had been well fed, we were to go to him.

It was a good meal and we were glad of it. When we had finished we went straight to the provincial's room where we found him waiting for us. He was a man who did not waste words and so, after blessing us, he bade us tell him everything about our journey and what we had found at Sandomierz.

We had hardly begun, however, when he interrupted to tell us to wait awhile for he wanted a written account. While he sent Father Nicholas for the librarian, he and I set a table with candles, pens, ink and parchment. As soon as Nicholas had returned with the librarian, he told the latter to sit down and write a short summary of what we were telling him.

'Be careful to make it short,' he told him, 'and above all, be sure that you put in nothing that people might cavil at.'

So we sat at the other side of the room in the dusk lit only by the flickering light of the candle on the librarian's table, and told the provincial our story, pretty much as I have already written it, and afterwards he questioned us. I took my share in the telling as far as our experiences on the journey and in the church went; but I said nothing, of course, of my vigil on the night before we left. Now, after all these years when, by experience, I have tested the truth of my train of reasoning and the conclusions I drew from it as I knelt at the foot of the crucifix, it does not matter what I write, for it is an old man's tale of a young one. But then I was still working out the sequence of my ideas and I had not yet put them to the test. After all that night is many years old, and it only represented a beginning of what I have been trying to practice ever since.

When we had finished our tale and answered the provincial's questions, the librarian was told to read to us what he had written and we were asked whether we agreed with it as a true summary. When a couple of fair copies had been made, I asked for and obtained the original which I insert here, so that you may see for yourselves by reading it that the provincial did not send an exaggerated account to Rome. It was put in one package with a copy of the letter we had received from the Subprior at Sandomierz, and both were sent to the General together.

'The happy day dawned when the friars of Saint Mary Magdalen's priory were to be freed from their bodily prison. The blood-thirsty Scythians rushed in like fierce lions, and Sadoc the shepherd and his devoted flock of friars were slain in the church itself, while they were singing their swan-song, the *Salve Regina*. A certain friar, however, who had hidden himself in the upper part of the church, when he heard them singing, came down and offered his throat to the sword of the Scythians, and so he joined himself to the company of friars ascending into heaven, which was resounding with thy sweet song, O Blessed Virgin Mary.'

One could not say that there was any exaggeration of facts, but the whole seemed to me a little flowery, and this floweriness obscured the stark reality of what we saw at Sandomierz. It was obvious that both the provincial and the librarian were exulting in the martyrdom of their fellow countrymen, and rejoicing at the thought of forty-nine more friars interceding for them in heaven; so, if the librarian's pen ran away with him a little and the provincial made no objection to the flowery language, the whole thing was quite understandable and quite easy to excuse.

Next morning the provincial assembled the community in the chapter room, and Nicholas and I had to repeat our story and answer the questions put to us. Later on, in the cloister, different men came to us, singly and in groups and asked many more questions. They were all acquainted with the priory of Saint Mary Magdalen and wanted to know more details: how the

Scythians had left the church and priory, in complete ruin or reparable; whether the Blessed Sacrament had been saved from profanation and so on. Besides this, most of them had friends among the community and wanted to know if we had been able to recognize them, what they looked like and any other detail we could give. After all it is no small thing to have a friend a saint and a martyr. Many of them ended their questioning with a sigh and a shrug of their shoulders.

'I suppose we are not worthy of martyrdom and that is why the Scythians did not come to Kracow' was the remark we heard many times over.

The next day the provincial sent for me.

'There will be an opportunity for you to return to England next week, Thomas,' he said. 'You have made yourself a useful member of the community while you have been here, and I could find plenty more work for you to do if you were staying on. I think you have made good progress in the study of humanity, the reason for your coming'—here he smiled—'How should you feel about it if I were to ask your provincial to give you to us for the Polish Province? For one thing'—here he smiled again—'it is easier to attain to martyrdom here than it is in England.'

I stood for a moment thinking. I had been very happy in Poland. Martyrdom was an attraction. I should be following in the footsteps of Sadoc and Kazemierz, and Jasek would be there beyond the grave waiting for me. But then, on the other hand, what right had I to choose for myself the road I should take to heaven? How could I be certain that, in any self-chosen path, my courage would be equal to the struggle; to a violent death, such as Augustine's for instance. By taking God's way as it was shown me by my superiors, I should be certain of the grace to do what he asked of me. I should have no such guarantee if I made my own choice.

Most important of all, since the dedication of myself I made at Sandomierz, when I had realized what such a dedication implied, I was Christ's man, pledge to follow him to my life's end; and it belonged to him to choose the manner of my following; even if it meant Anzelinus' way, Margaret's way, or the way that has been mine and is now nearing its end: a life of preaching to the poor, and now to sit useless in the infirmary with a gangrenous leg.

I looked across at the provincial.

'I leave it to you and to my provincial in England to settled that matter,' I answered; and laughed a little from sheer lightness of heart to think that I had no right to make so momentous a choice, and that whichever way it was made the grace of obedience would be mine.

'Then, in that case,' said the provincial, 'I'll not take the responsibility of asking for you, much as I'd like to keep you, but I'll send you back.'

So I packed my knapsack and early in the following week I said good-bye to my Polish friends. I went back to Danzig by boat just as I had come three years previously. We made a stop and moored the boat to the quay at Sandomierz, just as we had before and I went ashore for an hour or so to the Priory of Saint Mary Magdalen, to pray in the church of Saint Mary.

They were repairing the church and putting everything in order, and some of the friars from Saint James were there, superintending and helping with the work. I spoke to one or two whom I had known, and what they said was an echo of what I had heard at Kracow.

'Why were we not judged worthy to share their passion?'

The story of the martyrdom had brought many young men to join the Order. There was a temporary novitiate at Saint James, but they hoped before long to open that at Saint Mary Magdalen again. It would not be necessary to finish all the repairs. The novices could be put to work.

Before I left I went to the crucifix behind the pillar at the bottom of the church and there I renewed my dedication. I asked the loving Mother of God and our Mother, the Magdalen, Sadoc and his companions to intercede for me; and I made a special petition to my friend, Kazemierz, to remember me so that, even if I should go astray, I might find my way back at last, as he had. Then comforted and strengthened, I returned to the boat.

On we went towards the river mouth and Danzig; and for the last time I saw the endless plain and listened to the clank of the wooden wheels as they turned in every village, bringing buckets of water from the wells. The men sang as they rowed. And I listened to the patterned harmony of men and machinery; land and water.

I left the boat at Danzig and the Dominicans in the priory there gave me a great welcome. They had heard rumors of the massacre at Sandomierz, and when they learnt that I had been to the priory and had seen what had happened, they did not rest until I had given them every detail. I had been there no longer than a week when the prior learnt of a ship sailing to the port of London, and when the Master heard where I had been there was no difficulty about my having a free passage.

There is no need for me to write about the voyage, for I did not make much of it. I was quite as seasick as I had been three years previously. Almighty God did not intend men to make a sailor of me and only too well I knew it.

I reached London one afternoon a week later and after inviting the ship's master to visit us in Holborn as soon as he was free to do so, I went straight to the priory. Everything in the city looked little and cramped after the great spaces in which I had spent the past three years. But it was home nevertheless.

The provincial was in residence, I remember. I have reasons for remembering that it was Simon de Hinton, the man who was deposed in the following year by the General Chapter held at Barcelona, for refusing to accept foreign students at Oxford. The next after him—and I am sure it was not he whom I met on my return—was Robert Kilwardby, who was later made Archbishop of Canterbury.

Out of the fog of my homecoming, I seem to remember hearing the people say as I came along the streets that our King Henry had not long returned from France, where he had offered homage to the French king for Gascoigny; and they seemed angry about it. It was all strange, almost as if one had been taken out of one picture and put into another, where one could not find one's surroundings.

And so, beyond disconnected tags and odds and ends, I remember little about my actual return to England, except that I stumbled into the priory, and people seemed to crowd around me and ask questions. And I could tell them nothing except that I was tired and sick, and if I might go to sleep now, I would tell them everything in the morning.

Then the provincial suddenly appeared out of nowhere, and after he had blessed me, he told them to let me rest and he would see me when I had shaken the sleep off me.

And that is all I remember.

CHAPTER XXV

The End of My Story

I have an impression that the provincial sent for me next day; but it may have been two or three days later, for I remember that my mind was clear, so that I must have been well rested.

'Well, Thomas!' he said. 'We are glad to have you back. What about your studies?'

I told him that I had spent my first winter at the Studium in Prague, studying under a pupil of Master Albert's, and that, besides philosophy, we had had lectures in natural science, which we had taken in a new way that our lecturer, Friar Albert, said he had learnt from his master. The provincial asked what I had done in the matter of languages; and I told him that I was reasonably fluent in Lingua Franca, that I had some knowledge of Polish and Hungarian, and had a smattering of Arabic.

'Anything else?' asked the provincial.

I hesitated a moment. 'The Polish provincial said that I had made reasonably good progress in the study of humanity,' I answered, wondering whether the prior had told him why he sent me and if that was what he wanted to hear.

'Good,' he said; then suddenly he leant back and went on in quite a different tone: 'Now, tell me all about your three years abroad. I want to hear everything. Sit down, and take your time.' As I settled myself on a stool, he remarked: 'I am sending you at once to Oxford, to study for your Master's degree and teach as lector.'

So that is to be my way, I thought, and I found it a pleasant one, for I have always been interested in study and teaching.

Then I began to tell the provincial of all that had happened since I left London. I gave him the facts quite briefly but, somehow, though I had not meant to do so, I found myself telling him at greater length my thoughts and the conclusions I had drawn from all I had seen and heard; and how, before the crucifix at Sandomierz, all my doubts and difficulties had been resolved. How I now understood that the real following of Christ was something quite different from what my fancy had painted it; and how I was now ready to be Christ's man to my life's end. I told him about Albert and Kazemierz and Anzelinus and Margaret and Augustine; and how, at first, I had found their actual lives filled with failure and humiliation to be in utter discord with what I had conceived the following of Christ to mean; the Hero of my imagination raised on high. I told him how I now understood all these apparent discords to be part of a great heavenly harmony which was resolved into unison at the foot of the cross.

The provincial sat listening to me, and from beginning to end he did not say one word. Even when I had come to the end of my story still he said nothing but: 'Thank you, Thomas.'

And then we sat silent for quite a long while, and I looked out over the cloister garden, going over and over in my mind all that I had told the provincial and wondering why I had told him. I could find no reason except that, after three years, I, an Englishman, was talking to an Englishman in my own language, and this, to quote a tag of Saxon poetry, had loosened the bonds of my thought my 'broest-horde.'

At last, quite suddenly, he stood up and I got to my feet also.

'I've changed my mind about sending you to Oxford,' he said. 'I am going to make you a preacher, not a teacher. You go anywhere that your prior sends you, of course, but, unless he gives you special instructions to go elsewhere, you will make East Anglia your circuit.' It was not until a long time afterwards that I learnt why the provincial had changed his mind, and this explains how I know he was Simon de Hinton. He was determined not to allow foreign Dominicans to study in our house at Oxford, why I do not know. But, hearing how much affection and reverence I felt for the Poles and Hungarians, and how ready and anxious I was to return the kindness they had shown me, he was afraid lest I should influence the community at Oxford against his wishes. I should not have done so intentionally, of course, but I might easily have brought my influence to bear in favor of foreign students, through the very fact that I was so grateful to my friends of the past three years;

and the influence I brought to bear might have been the more powerful from the fact that I had no intention of going contrary to the provincial's wishes.

I made the *Venia* and left the room, and a few days later I took to the road.

For nearly thirty years I have travelled for nine or ten months in each year; my only break being when I have stayed several times in the year at one or other of our priories; but never for more than a few weeks at a time. I have preached in cathedrals and in village churches, on the steps of market-crosses and on village greens. As far as I could I have tried to be just what I was born to be: one of the people. Above all, I have loved children and I think they have counted me as a friend.

It has been a happy and a blessed life, looking outward and forward in my effort to follow Christ. He has always been before me, just beyond my reach, but he is always on the level where I can try to catch up with him. In my hours of weariness, or when things have gone awry, I have always known that he is there, on his cross, not much higher than I am. He is my Brother, and as brothers we have shared everything.

I have always grasped this with my understanding and tried to adhere to it with my will; but my senses have seldom had any part in the matter. I have done my best to follow reason, but have paid as little heed as possible to what I feel. This is what I think should be the mental and spiritual outlook of an ordinary Friar Preacher; and I am a very ordinary one, busy among the poor and unlearned.

And now, just as I have finished this manuscript and carried out as well as I could the prior's wishes, though at times the pain has made it difficult, the infirmarian has been in to tell me that the prior is going to give me the Last Sacraments.

Please God, it will not be long before, by his great mercy, I find myself in purgatory; safe on my way to join Jasek and Sadoc and Kazemierz at the Feet of my Master.

Frater Thomas Fretum, Ordinis Praedicatorum.

About the Author

Sister Mary Catherine Anderson, O.P. was born Kathleen Agnes Cicely Anderson on January 21, 1888 in Falmouth, Cornwall, England. Born to an Anglican clergyman, Kathleen converted with her family to the Catholic Church when still a little girl. She was educated by the Stone Dominican Sisters at their convent of St Marychurch and entered the congregation on May 2, 1908 at St Dominic's Convent, Stone, receiving the religious name of Sister Mary Catherine. Sister made her profession on November 25 1909 and afterwards trained as a primary school teacher at the Sacred Heart Training College in St Charles's Square, London.

By 1936, when Sister was assigned to St Marychurch, she had begun to write—mainly historical novels of the revolts in Devon and Cornwall. It is during this time that Sister wrote her most popular book, *Brother Petroc's Return,* which received great acclaim in both England and America. Following this came many other titles including two biographies—*Steward of Souls* and *A Treasure of Joy and Gladness*—as well as lives of St Margaret of Hungary and St Hyacinth.

After her retirement she was appointed prioress to the community in Kelvedon, Essex and then assigned to the convent in Brewood where she continued to write. She died at Stone on April 14, 1972 in the 85th year of her life and the 63rd year of religious profession.

www.ingramcontent.com/pod-product-compliance
Lightning Source LLC
Chambersburg PA
CBHW051950220626
47052CB00004B/878